Stephen blocked Nina at the door.

> He said: What are you doing home?
> She said: My cold got worse, so I took
> the rest of the day off.
> He said: Me too . . . but I brought my
> work home with me.

She looked past him into the bedroom they shared
. . . and there was his beautiful secretary. Dressed,
but just barely. Lawyer Stephen Blume had more
work to do the next morning—handling his own
divorce.

When Nina stopped being Blume's wife, she became
his obsession—a mad passion neither sex nor psy-
chiatry could still. He watched her, followed her,
even made friends with her hippie lover just to get
close to her. He was nutty with desire, crazy with
yearning. He was BLUME IN LOVE.

Blume In Love

A Novelization by

JOSH GREENFELD

Written for the screen and directed by

PAUL MAZURSKY

**WARNER
PAPERBACK
LIBRARY**

A Warner Communications Company

WARNER PAPERBACK LIBRARY EDITION

First Printing: August, 1973
Second Printing: September, 1973
Third Printing: December, 1973

Warner Paperback Library is a division of Warner Books, Inc.
75 Rockefeller Plaza, New York, N.Y. 10019.

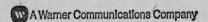 A Warner Communications Company

To Paul

In friendship

Any man who'd rape his own wife
would father his own child.

1

Don't call me Blume. Call me Stephen. Or even Steve. But not Blume. It's not that I hate my name—in fact, I rather like it. Blume: you have to pucker up your lips as if to kiss in order to say it. And once you say it, it lingers on your lips with a note of resonance. Blume-m-m-m-m-m. But I dislike patronyms alone; they're so patronizing, they reek of officialdom and condescension and impersonality. High-school teachers I hated most used to call me Blume. The people in college I could stand the least used to call me Blume. And Nina, when she wanted to deny the fact that we had ever existed together, would try to make it seem as if I never existed at all for her by calling me Blume. Just Blume.

But I do exist. I'm alive in Venice. Each day I come to the Piazza San Marco. I count the pigeons, I drink coffee, and I think. There are a lot of pigeons. Yesterday I counted up to 819 before I lost my place. I drink a lot of coffee: a half dozen saucers sometimes pile up next to me. But I usually think about just one thing: love.

So today I brought this notebook with me. I've decided the only way to stop thinking about love is to start writing about everything else. As a therapy. Only I feel the way I used to when confronted with empty bluebooks in college final exams waiting to be filled with answers to essay questions I couldn't make sense of, let alone begin to answer. SHOW HOW EVENTS IN IRELAND, FRANCE, OR THE UNITED STATES AFFECTED BRITISH HISTORY. OR SHOW HOW EVENTS IN GREAT BRITAIN AFFECTED IRISH, FRENCH OR AMERICAN HISTORY. CHOOSE TWO OUT OF THREE COUN-

9

TRIES AND DESCRIBE FULLY GERMANY'S RE-
ACTIONS.

Let me describe myself: I'm thirty-two, white, Cau-
casian. I have blond hair, brown eyes, a beard. When
last seen, I was wearing chukka boots, a suede jacket, and
flare slacks. I have sometimes been accused of being hand-
some by innocent bystanders, but I myself wouldn't swear
to it under oath. And I still can't help thinking about just
one thing: love.

On the way over here this morning I passed the Ducal
Palace. I leaned against a colonnade, my arms folded,
stared out at the water, and tried to think about something
else. Anything else. I got myself to concentrate on the fact
that Venice is sinking into the sea, so many inches per
year, and thought that eventually all the magic and the
beauty of this place would be gone. And then I thought
about California and how just as surely one day the San
Andreas Fault would open up all the way and that would
be gone, too: the terrible smog, the incredible freeway
traffic, and even the Lakers. And I was beginning to feel
more sorry for the world—or at least its geography—than
for myself.

Suddenly I heard a sound. I thought someone was softly
calling: Blume. Blume. Blume. It came from the other side
of the colonnade. I slowly peeked around like a child playing hide-and-seek, wanting to see but wary of being seen.
There were two young Italian lovers, a boy and a girl, who
couldn't have been more than twenty. The sounds I'd heard
were their passionate coos—and cues; his face was touching hers, and he was about to kiss her. Then he saw something that obviously disturbed him. He leaned past her face
and bent his head around the colonnade to get a better
look at what was disturbing him: me.

I was caught in the act like a Peeping Tom. I turned
around and walked away. But from that moment on, I
could only see the passing lovers in the crowd, the pairs
and couples, and all the other pedestrians as solitary as
myself faded away. And I smiled at them before they could
glare back at me. Lovers in every possible permutation and
combination:

10

An old man poking along over the cobblestones with a mahogany cane, a woman almost as old holding to his other arm as if for dear life.

A fat lady carrying a huge shopping bag containing, no doubt, bundles of pasta and a little tiny transistorized man wearing a straw hat staring idolatrously up into her eyes as if she were Sophia Loren herself.

A father carrying on his shoulders a little blond girl with long hair, wiggling and jiggling her while she bounced and laughed.

A man in a business suit, a woman in a miniskirt, arms around each other, strolling knee to knee, hip to hip, eyes completely riveted on each other. So totally in love.

There's no way out of it, I guess: love is a miracle. It's like a birthmark. You can't hide it. You can't hide from it. When you see two people in love, somehow you feel a little bit of it yourself.

Like those people three tables over from me in the café where I'm sitting now. He must be about sixty: gray hair, fat cheeks, big rings on his fingers. She's no more than twenty: great bra-less boobs in a tie-dye knit blouse, long lovely legs in hip-high boots with just enough flesh showing for dramatic contrast. Absolutely stunning. He reaches across the table and takes her hand. Now he's rubbing it softly, gently. She's looking a him respectfully, worshipfully. And he leans across the table and kisses her on the cheek. And she bends over and smooches on his hand. Lovely.

Obviously, there's no age limit, either, when it comes to love. That man knows what love is. Sure, it's possible that he is thinking of bed. But the feeling is more than just sexual. I can tell by his eyes. They glow more with passion than with lechery. I think.

But why am I being such a puritan? What's wrong with bed? And sex? Because if that can't be love, nothing is. How else can you express all the emotions that have built up in you? How else can you turn violence into tenderness? How else can you get so close to another person that you almost merge and feel all but one? And where else can you get such a fantastic thrill?

Making love to someone you love, there's nothing like it. Making love to someone you don't love, that isn't so bad, either. Not being able to make love to someone you don't love, that's an awful bummer. But not being able to make love to someone you love, that's the greatest torture in the world.

Fortunately, somehow Venice brings out the love in lovers. People who might be a little shy back in America seem to lose their inhibitions here. Like that middle-aged American couple now looking for a table, trying to decide where to sit down. He's got the camera strapped to his chest. She's got the guidebooks. He looks like he calls her "Mother" and she answers him back "Father" and she's Eastern Star and he's American Legion. Back home they eat hot cereal for breakfast and she's never said the word *fuck* in her life. He sells insurance, mostly car or home-owner, or runs a hardware store and hasn't missed a high school football game in fifteen years. She bakes like a whiz and sends out each Christmas a long letter instead of a card bringing everyone up to date on all the "doings" in the family. They came on a package tour and went to Hawaii two years ago. (I can tell that by his shirt.) They have 2.7 kids—the .7 kid being the one who is away at college or in the service. And they worry about him—or her—a great deal, wondering about all the new freedoms of the younger generation, comparing it to "their day," and agreeing that perhaps it's all going too far.

But this is Venice: they're holding hands. And she's casually rubbing his hand against the outside of her thigh. And any minute now she just might as casually give him the shock—and thrill—of his middle-aged life by quietly suggesting: "Herbert, let's fuck."

Love puts you through many changes, has many shapes and forms. Take those two women I see sitting at the table up against the wall. One is wearing a tweed suit, oxford shoes, and fedora; her dark, stringy hair is cut short, too. The other woman is very slender, fragile, with wispy sandy hair, a patrician nose, and long, tapered fingers. The Tweed Suit is smoking a Schimmel-Pennick cigar and Long Tapered Fingers has a long tapered cigarette holder.

They're holding hands, too. And it's easy to assume that Tweed Suit is the butch and Long Tapered Fingers is the femme in an old-fashioned lesbian relationship. But nothing in love is ever that simple. Nobody ever knows exactly what goes on between any two people—sometimes even when you're one of them. Sure, those two are women in Love. But maybe it's Long Tapered Fingers who puts the screws to Tweed Suit every night and their dress and manner are just a game they play because of the game society plays, holding up one form of love above all others.

Those two hippies in front of me, on the other hand, have nothing to hide. They're both in jeans, and sweat shirts, and have long flowing hair, and are barefoot. If it wasn't for his mustache and beard, he could be her. And as they sit there, their eyes never leaving each other, it's as if they were the only couple in the café. In the piazza. In Venice. In Italy. In all the world. They almost look stoned. But they're just high on each other.

I know what they're feeling—*I even feel their feeling*—the feeling is the same in all of us. It makes the blood rush. The heart beats faster. Reason vanishes.

I can even see it at this minute happening to someone else. There is a heavyset man in a dark coat with a fur collar sitting at a table diagonally across from me. He looks like an actor from some old Visconti flick. He is stirring his espresso endlessly; his head is poking forward nervously like a turkey's; his blubber lips are parted and moist. I can almost hear his breathing, I can all but see the beads of his salivation. He is staring shamelessly, unremittingly, at the head of a beautiful young golden boy with clear, smooth, delicate skin. The boy is other-worldly. He could be twelve, he could be twenty. He is with an older woman—perhaps his mother, perhaps an aunt. He seems oblivious of her. But he is also oblivious of the Visconti actor. The Visconti actor is somehow straining to get his attention, trying to send out psychic waves so that the golden boy will turn around. The golden boy still does not even notice him, spoons fastidiously from a dish of ice cream. This is driving the Visconti actor wild. I think he's going to jump out of his seat any minute now like a jack-in-the-box. But no, I see what he's doing instead. His hand has fallen into his lap, he's gradually slinking a bit more under the table, he's cocking his head to one side, his eyes never wavering for an instant from the golden boy, his mouth opening even wider. *The son-of-a-bitch is jerking off!*

But I guess that's love, too. Whenever passion reigns supreme. And you feel *alive*—even if a little soggy, afterwards.

2

I've just reread what I wrote yesterday. I can see how this notebook is going to be even more like therapy than I expected. I'm going to fiddle-faddle and doodle-daddle and talk about everything else except what's really on my mind. But that's why I started to write here in the first place: to get my mind off what's on my mind. Because my mind is only on one thing all the time, and being in Venice doesn't help any. So let me order another espresso and try to get my head, if not my mind, together.

Espresso, to me, by the way, is the only really good coffee. Of course, it has to be made properly or it's a bummer. You need the best coffee, the best machine . . . and a good stomach. It's a perfect way to start the day and the only way to end the night. The only problem is that you have to order it.

The waiter and I go through a routine here every day that is predictably unpredictable. I never know whether he's putting me *on* or *down*. It varies every time. Like I'm going to hold up my hand now, catch his eye, point to my empty cup, and then write down exactly what happens.

He saw me. He nodded. (I even think there was a trace of a smile on his thin lips beneath his pencil-line mustache.) He disappeared in the back. He came out again with a cup of espresso on his silver tray. He served it to me. And bowed.

"Grazie," I said. *"Grazie."*

"You are welcome," he shot back in perfect English, as if he had been sitting in the House of Lords all his life.

"Thank you," I replied.

"Prego," he said. And took game, set, and match point.

15

Funny, my thinking about tennis. I haven't played tennis in three months. But maybe it's because I'm developing a tennis elbow. A psychosomatic tennis elbow. Unless you can get a tennis elbow from drinking espresso.

That waiter! If I was an Italian, I bet he would have answered me in Italian.

Pardon me now while I begin to cry. I can't help it. I can't hold it in any longer. I've got to let it all out. In tears. What's primed my gushers is the sight of a pretty blonde who's just passed by. The sight of her made my heart leap up faster than the pigeons scattering before her. Being over-caffeinated didn't help any, either. And now I've had the pang of a letdown and the full brunt of the realization of how badly I miss Nina, of how much I need Nina.

Nina is a blonde. The same type. Even though there's only one Nina. And I'm in love with Nina. Oh God, am I in love with Nina. That's my tragedy! God, how I love her! And seeing that blonde didn't make it any easier.

I know I may sound like an acned juvenile or a marsh-mallow-popping adolescent. But love is love, as I've been trying to say, whether you're six or sixty. And so any of the usual nonsense about acting your age has absolutely no relevancy. And just as nothing on the face of this earth can give greater pleasure than love, nothing can bring you down further, either. If I'm an allegedly grown man sitting at a café table in the middle of the Piazza San Marco at high noon crying his fucking heart out, so be it. But I also might cite the fact that there is a mitigating circumstance in my particular case. To be in love with a woman who scorns you is a problem. To be in love with a man who scorns you is a dilemma. But to be in love with your own ex-wife is a tragedy!

To look at me, my shoulders racking convulsively, my espresso cup and saucer askew, the tears still streaming down my cheeks unabated, one would never guess who I am or what I do. My fellow tourists must all assume I'm off on some special trip American Express didn't tell them about. My Italian comrades-in-espresso, on the other hand,

16

probably feel as if they have misread me, that beneath my calm North American exterior lurks a volatile Latino temperament. But the only concern that really enters my mind at the moment is this: if Nina were here right now, what would she say? What would she do? Would she take me in her arms and console me soothingly? Or would she walk right past me as imperviously as the blonde whose passage reminded me of her in the first place? And isn't that the height of weirdness and craziness itself—my thinking of Nina as the one person who can console me for thinking of her?

I'm not going to look at people any more. Instead, I'll look at the pigeons. Pigeons aren't people; people couldn't get by on just a steady diet of pigeon food. Unless the pigeon food were peanuts and the people were teenagers. But I wonder how the pigeons feel about having to eat pigeon food sold by a human being. You never see a pigeon selling pigeon food. It's always a member of an outside species exploiting their appetites. Pigeons should have the right to operate the pigeon-food concessions in their own communities. Pigeon power! Pigeon capitalism! It's the only way they can get ahead, go on up in the world. They should become militant, stage demonstrations, set up picket lines, shit on people everywhere. They should also have a good hot-breakfast program for the young pigeons. The trouble is, they don't have a leader, a dynamic spokesman. They need a Huey Pigeon. An Eldridge Pigeon. A Martin Luther Pigeon.

Instead there is only the honky Walter Pidgeon.

All power to the pigeons! And fuck all the seagulls, too!

But the Piazza San Marco is no place to start a pigeon revolution. These pigeons are too well fed, they're all so fat. They can't even hop right; they seem to wobble toward all those handfuls of pigeon food tossed at them. They remind me of the people in the waiting room of my office in Beverly Hills.

People! I'm back to people. And in another moment I'll be thinking of Nina and breaking up again. I'd better brace myself with another espresso.

This time when the waiter brought me my espresso I thought I was playing it very cool.

I said, "Thank you."

He nodded. *"Prego."*

So I came back, *"Grazie."*

He bowed. "You are welcome." And won again. Where did he learn to be so smart? In the Italian Army?

The sun has broken through the clouds, the musicians are setting up for the afternoon concert, it's going to be a glorious day after all, and I think I can even face my own music now: fill these pages with what fills my head, write about myself and Nina.

Nina and I were married for six years, two months, and eleven days. I was doing very well as a divorce lawyer in Beverly Hills. It's not hard to do well as a divorce lawyer in Beverly Hills. The clients flock to your office—like pigeons. And all you have to do is calm them down and ask them to be their normally reasonable selves. Which is sometimes difficult, but rarely impossible. A divorce is really basically much simpler to work out than a marriage. After all, a marriage is traditionally conceived of as something that is supposed to last forever, while a divorce is expected to last no longer than the next marriage. Yet, ironically, a marriage costs less than eight dollars in fees while a divorce can cost whatever the lawyer has the nerve to charge. And we lawyers are nervy, especially as we get more successful. Oh, we always know how to justify ourselves, that's part and parcel of our training. We say we're like doctors, charging what the traffic will bear in one area so that we can offer our services in other areas more freely. To Civil Rights. To Minority Groups. To Indigent Movie Stars. But the fact remains that we always take more for ourselves, in glory or coin, than we ever donate to others. We take the cream; we give back the skimmed milk. We're adjusted, we're adult; the things we do are far removed from the things we wanted to do.

I was the guy who was always organizing protest meetings, giving out leaflets, writing editorials when I was a student. As a lawyer I preside over the division of communal property, arrange for the custody of children, settle back-alimony disputes. I've been involved with the Grape Workers and the California Democratic Council and the Peace Movement, but it was always something somehow social—extracurricular, something I did after work, not in my own prime time, so to speak.

Nina, on the other hand, has always been involved fully, completely. There is never anything halfway about her. At the age of twenty-nine, she still cares for people on a real basis, the way most of us do at the age of nineteen abstractedly. She was always raising money for some cause or another—or giving our money away to it. And she would work hard at her job, often putting in extra hours, just so she could help people out. I couldn't have lasted a single day at her job. It would have knocked me out completely. But Nina was always too busy to even begin to become disillusioned. Disappointed, yes. Disillusioned, never.

She worked for the County Welfare Office in Venice. Venice, California. I don't know if they have a welfare office here in Venice, Italy. Frankly, I don't know if they need one. The only welfare they could need here is for the slower pigeons. And maybe the city can use some supplementary support so it doesn't slip off into the water forever.

I remember the first time we sailed into Venice, Nina and I. This Venice, I mean. Venice, Italy. We were on a Greek ship and had been on a tour of the Aegean Islands. Andros. Tinos. Mikonos. Mikonos was the place that really got us—all those white windmills, the lovely expanse of beach. We decided someday we'd come back and live there. But then it was the same way when we reached the Adriatic Sea and sailed up the shoreline of Yugoslavia. We thought we'd never find a harbor as beautiful as the Bay of Dubrovnik.

But we were wrong. When we came to Venice, it was as if our whole honeymoon trip up to that point had been but a prelude, a preliminary hearing. I first sensed this at dockside; we were both awed into silence.

"What do you think?" I finally said.

Nina breathed deeply and squeezed my hand. She watched the green-aproned porters scrambling about the cobblestoned street, loading luggage, calling out the names of the hotels they represented. She looked up and saw the skyline of spires and turrets, the mosque and cathedral heritages commingling colorfully in the gray, moist air. And in front of us was a canal, gondolas gliding by in graceful, lyric swoops while vaporettos steamed past them with prosaic mass-transit purposefulness.

I had been to Venice before. I knew the magic of the city, the fact that it was real and make-believe at the same time—or as real as a fairy tale one was willing to believe in.

When we got to our hotel I registered and tipped the porter for our luggage. Then I motioned to Nina. "Come."

"Where?"

"You'll see."

She took my arm and we left the hotel and began to walk through the streets of Venice. Some I remembered, some were unfamiliar. We walked past shops selling exquisite glass, Florentine leather, perfectly wrought cameos, Etruscan jewelry. We crossed and recrossed canals just so we could look at the bridges we had been on a moment before. It didn't seem as if I knew where I was going, as if we were another tourist couple strolling aimlessly, any lovers happy to be walking anywhere together. But I was heading us toward the Piazza San Marco. And the moment I heard the strains of music, the afternoon concert in performance, I knew I had steered us in the right direction. We walked toward the sound of the music, our arms now about each other's waist.

We came to the familiar corner and I stopped. "Ready?" I asked Nina.

She nodded her head slowly, solemnly. "Ready," she said.

I walked away from her and caught her hand in mine and led her as if I were an usher, the music swelling almost on cue, into Piazza San Marco. It was the first time Nina had ever seen it—the churches, the banners, the tourists, the pigeons, like ten football fields laid out end to end, side to side, teeming with halftime pageant shows going on all at once. There is no other sight like it in the world: it is as if the world itself were created by a designer of wedding cakes and you only had to poke anywhere to taste something sweet. At the same time, you feared that if you tried to taste it, it would all crumble. And that was part of the attraction, the obvious vulnerability of it all.

Nina stood there, gulping, swallowing for air, nodding. And then the sun came out, warmly intensifying what was already almost too vivid, too fine to bear. A cardinal passed us, his red robe trailing, a cluster of pigeons following behind as if they were footmen. A gray-haired woman wearing a black lace shawl appeared, began to whistle softly, and soon dozens of cats materialized, ready to be fed. A man on a white horse, a fourteenth-century duke in brilliant green tights and golden jacket, rode across the square toward a motion-picture crew brandishing aluminum reflectors.

It was that make-believe reality that is always so overwhelming. I turned to look at Nina again. Her eyes had reddened, she was blinking back tears, and she was just about to begin to shake. I took her in my arms and held her as tightly as I could. And she held me back.

Then we stepped apart, and she blew her nose. I bought some pigeon food. And we sprinkled handfuls beside us as we strolled toward the outdoor café.

"I think," Nina said after a while, a slight vibrato in her voice, "I think the only time I ever felt like this . . ." And she trailed off, lost or overcome by reverie.

I pointed toward an empty table and we sat down.

"Don't laugh," she said earnestly, her face threatening to break into a scowl, "at what I'm going to say."

"I won't," I promised.

She inhaled deeply. "The only other time I felt like this," her eyes sparkled, a smile of contentment flashed across her lips, "was the first time I had sex."

A waiter came to our table and bowed.

"What would you like to have, Nina?" I asked.

"Sex," she said.

I looked up to see if the waiter had overheard. He

seemed to be studying a pigeon about to land atop a ledge in the distance.

"Due espresso, per favore," I ordered.

He looked at me, a mischievous look in his eyes. "Two espressos. Thank you, sir," he said. In perfect English.

I tried to stare him down but he didn't bat an eyelash. *"Prego,"* I finally nodded. He bowed, swept up the menus, and turned away. And I thought I could see his shoulders tweaking, as if he were containing laughter, holding it back, as he walked toward the espresso machine.

"They all speak English," I complained to Nina.

Nina was still looking out at the piazza, her eyes watery, her lovely boobies rising and falling like billowing waves, her cashmere sweater becoming a beckoning ocean of fleece proclaiming extraordinary tactile sensations.

She took my hand and played with my longest finger, rubbing it ever so softly. Her tongue massaged her own lips; her mouth was half opened. "I love you," she said, making not the slightest effort to lower her voice a decibel beneath its normal pitch.

"I love you," I answered back. The string section in the orchestra seemed to be eavesdropping; the violinists all dipped their instruments our way as if they were as capable of flight as pigeons that hopped across the pavement.

Nina's tongue shot out from her half-opened mouth and wiggled from side to side. This time when she spoke there was an unnatural hoarseness to her voice. "Let's go back to the hotel," she breathed.

"Now?"

She was rising before I could answer, taking my hand to lead me out of the piazza just as I had led her in. My knees began to feel woozy as I caught her excitement. The music swelled romantically, and I was sure someone in the orchestra was a lip-reader. "I think they must know." I pointed toward the orchestra.

The waiter appeared with our espressos; he did not even seem to notice that Nina was standing. He deposited the coffees, spilling some espresso on the tab in the saucer. I picked up the moist tab and dropped at least a hundred extra lire on his tray. It was no time for me to count straight.

"Keep the change," I smiled at the waiter.

"Grazie," he replied. *"Grazie."*

Nina and I were possessed that moment, that day, that week in Venice with that feeling that people, lucky people, get only once or twice in a lifetime. We had great fucking before our honeymoon trip to Venice and we had great fucking after that during our six years, two months, and eleven days of marriage. But that zap, that sweet crazy zap, we had it all the time in Venice. We spent a week there. Half of the time in bed. All of it the most fantastic fucking imaginable.

There are things about Nina that remain marvelous mysteries to me to this day. To see her behind her desk at the County Welfare Office in Venice, all business and no nonsense, compassionate yet profoundly cool, interviewing welfare applicants—Chicanos and Blacks and Old People in shining dark clothing—arranging for Food Stamps, for Day Care, for Drug Treatments, for Hospital Admittance, for Visiting Nurses, you'd never guess what a reservoir of warmth and passion and good old-fashioned horniness resided within her. I guess to me that has always been one of her most attractive qualities, the fact that sex with Nina is not just one logical step more given her surface appearance, but a sudden and dramatic jump down—into another world that didn't seem possible with her. Her inaccessibility is part of her lure; that she seems so much in control makes getting her out of control so much more rewarding. Any tramp can fuck like a tramp. But Nina is such a lady that when she lets loose, the effect is mind-blowing. In bed Nina simply has no inhibitions at all, draws no lines anywhere, understands that preconceived definitions and restrictions remove the most joyous and creative aspects of lovemaking.

Naturally, I had trouble with the key when we got back to the hotel. It just wouldn't seem to turn the latch. I jiggled and jiggled, but nothing happened. I pulled the key out and shrugged helplessly at Nina. She looked down the corridor,

23

saw no one coming or going to the elevator, unzipped my fly, curled her hand around my cock, and kissed me in the ear, her tongue twirling, blowing gently in the way she knew I loved. I tried the key again, and this time it caught the tumblers easily. The door pushed open.

I slammed it behind me as we walked to the great fluffy eiderdown bed, Nina still holding my cock, not wanting to let go and my not wanting her to ever let go. We lay down on the bed, kicked off our shoes, kissed deeply, and my hand dipped beneath her slacks, below her mound, and found her cunt moist and waiting. I touched her clitoris, and she moaned and scratched my cock.

"No preliminaries?" I whispered into Nina's cheek.

"Shut up," she said. And bit my ear.

"I love you," I said.

"Shut up," she said.

I reached beneath her sweater and unhooked her brassiere, and then I rolled the sweater up over her head and removed the bra in one fluid motion. I buried my head between Nina's breasts, I sucked on her right nipple and I put my finger back in her cunt and stroked her at the same time. I pulled down her slacks and her panties, and she pushed them away with her toes.

I propped myself on my elbows and studied Nina's naked body as if I had never seen it before. I marveled again at her breasts; they were not big or overpowering boobs but nice, comfortable, perky, and alive tits; if she were to live to be a hundred, I decided, they would be impervious to age, always remain young and pubescent. And her skin was fair and smooth, but not so delicate that it could not wear a California sun-worshipper's coat of tan in places to contrast with her own natural pink whiteness. And her hair was natural, too, blond to the roots even at the dead-giveaway area beneath her mound. Nina was not pretty; she was beautiful.

I kissed Nina on one breast, then the other, twirling the nipples between my teeth. Then I blew on her cunt and kissed her there, my tongue darting in as far as it could.

"Are you cold?" I asked.

"I love you," she said.

24

"But I don't want you to catch cold."

"Shut up," she said.

I stood up to undress and Nina said, "Wait. Let me." And she got out of bed and rubbed her body up and down against mine, her bare breasts against my maroon turtleneck, her sun-tanned legs against my brown double-knit slacks, her wet snatch against the tip of my wallet sticking out of my back pocket; like a cat in heat she was touching me and rubbing up against me everywhere.

Then her rhythm abruptly changed. Slowly she peeled off my shirt. She kissed my hair and ran her tongue down my face and neck and chest until she came to my belt buckle. She unsnapped it, unfastened the waist button, and let my pants drop and slowly pulled down my jockey shorts. And then her tongue worked its way down my stomach past my cock up under my balls and around again until her lips slipped over my cock and her teeth squeezed gently on the tip and I felt her finger poking its way up my ass.

She steered me into bed, under the quilting, and we rolled there like little puppies, biting each other on the shoulders, our fingers moving everywhere. I slipped my cock in from the back, my hands clasped on her tits, and we lay there on our sides, moving slowly and slightly, ever so friendly. Then I pulled out to change to a more active position when Nina gently pushed my shoulders back and got on top, sliding down my cock, and began to ride in swirls, revolving about my cock like a planet around a sun, my cock boring deeper constantly like a drill. I could see Nina would be ready to come soon, so I turned her over and entered straight and hard to begin the final ride home. Her legs encased me, her arms enveloped me, her head rolled back and forth as she sweetly moaned while I thrust sharply, making each thrust feel as if it were the last one, but holding back, stopping, summoning up one more edge of control, and then thrusting even deeper than before until her body exploded in pleasure, her hands and arms massaging me gratefully, her lips searching for places to kiss, her voice breathlessly repeating: "Yes, Stephen. Yes. I love you. I love you. Stephen!"

"Shut up," I tried to say. But couldn't. For I was still stroking, thrusting, climbing plateau after plateau of pleasure, taking Nina with me for one more unendurable moment, emitting sigh-grunts of pleasure from the bottom of my throat to the roof of my mouth. I reached my hand farther under Nina, extending my finger, wiggling it up into her anus, and she responded digitally, doing the same to me, until scratching, screaming, biting, thrashing, in one great burst I came. And Nina came again with me, our motions not subsiding until every last drop oozed pleasurably from my cock, and we relaxed spent in each other's arms.

We kissed softly. "I love you," I said.

"What else is new?" Nina teased, her hand lightly scratching along my back.

"Oh, fuck you," I whispered.

"Please do," she said.

"Again?"

"Why not?"

"Right now?"

"Certainly, we're in the right position."

"I'm a little tired," I said.

"I'm not," she laughed. "Aren't I an animal?"

"Yes." I kissed her and began to withdraw, when suddenly her cunt became alive again, twisting and demanding, promising and imploring. And her fingers were probing everywhere.

"Do you think you can come one more time?" she asked earnestly.

"Only by memory," I said. And we were off again, my potency surprising me as much as it was pleasing both of us.

But that's how it was that holy, wonderful, crazy week of our honeymoon in Venice. Half the time we were in bed, half the time we were in the café in Piazza San Marco drinking espresso. Half the time we were acquisitive tourists watching the glass-blowers, picking up incredible bargains; half the time we were avaricious lovers twisting ourselves into unbelievable shapes and forms, fucking insatiably. Half the time we were at the Lido, gambling in

26

the Casino, dreaming of breaking the bank; half the time we were back at the hotel, gamboling all over the bed, somehow never getting overdrawn. No matter how you figure it, we did spend half our time fucking. My recuperative powers were amazing, and Nina never tired. And each fuck was better than the previous one, spurring us forever onward—and bedward. We were so full of love.

But then our honeymoon was over. And our marriage began.

3

I guess the difference between a honeymoon and a marriage is that a honeymoon is a dream—like Venice, Italy—and a marriage is real—like Venice, California. The trick is to make the marriage a dream, too. And I didn't think we were doing too badly until, of course, it was too late. Perhaps if it wasn't for Elmo we would still be married. Perhaps if it wasn't for Gloria we would never have split. Or perhaps a *different* Elmo or a Gloria would have come along anyway.

It's hard to keep any marriage going these days—especially in California. But we were managing to be one of the few young couples we knew that were still hanging in together. We'd have our battle royals and we needed counseling and therapy from time to time, but we were making it. Perhaps making it too well. Because after six years I had begun to take everything for granted, assumed our marriage would last forever, that nothing could break it apart. And all it took was a simple cold to wipe the whole slate away.

Plus the fact that Elmo was there waiting to move in. Elmo knew how to make anything into a dream. Nina met Elmo at work—he was one of her clients—and she took an exceptional interest in his case. After all, the County Welfare Office is a drab place and most of the people Nina had to deal with had the same dull, depressing stories to tell. But not Elmo. He was different. He was an original.

I can just see how it happened: the County Welfare Office in Venice jammed as usual with people waiting to be interviewed. Nina in her cubicle, nursing her cold, and trying to do her job at the same time. She's had a typical day: getting a transportation allowance for a retarded child so that his parents could afford to send him to a special school in Santa Monica. Putting some pressure on the office in Bay Street so they issued some food stamps to a family of seven that was trying to live on thirty-eight fifty a week. Arranging for a visiting nurse to check up on a diabetic old woman of seventy-eight living alone. And not even lunchtime yet.

Nina looked at the clock and saw there would be time possibly for just one more interview before the noon break. She picked the top gray folder out of the green steel tray on the right side of her desk, blew her stuffy nose, and went out to the benches in the waiting area, calling out the name on the folder: "Mr. Cole."

She looked around and no one seemed to rise, to be ready to follow her back, until a tall bearded man slowly unwrapped himself in the back row and stood up languidly. His hair was long, and he pushed it back and smiled beatifically at her, one hand cupping his chin. His clothes were as far-out as his expression: a Moroccan vest, an Indian bandana, tuxedo-striped trousers, and Western boots. Yet he moved with great dignity as he walked toward Nina, the smile never once leaving his lips.

"Mr. Cole?" Nina checked his name.

"Yes, ma'am, Elmo Cole." He nodded proudly, as if he were about to be awarded some great prize.

Nina touched her nose with a Kleenex. "Would you come with me, please," she said.

"Certainly, ma'am." Nina tried to place his speech, figure out what part of the country he came from. But it was difficult. He struck too cultured a note for a hillbilly, projected too much energy for an urban beat.

Elmo followed her down the long corridor, his heels clicking resonantly, to her office. She turned around once, and he smiled at her as if he had been expecting her to turn around at just that moment. In her office cubicle Nina pointed to an empty chair at the side of her desk. "Sit down, please."

She herself sat down behind her desk and wiped her nose again.

Elmo rubbed his hands over the top of his trousers, looked around the office as if its institutional décor were really esthetically interesting, and then leaned back, reached into his pocket, and extracted a muslin-packaged packet of Bull Durham. "Okay if I smoke?" he asked.

Nina was distracted. She had been glancing over his application form. "Yes, of course," she said, looking up at him impatiently.

He inclined his head toward her slightly and then rather elaborately, she thought, began the process of rolling a cigarette—producing the Zig-Zag paper, removing a sheet and creasing it, and then pouring the tobacco carefully along the fold.

"You want assistance, Mr. Cole?" she asked sharply.

"Yes," Elmo nodded.

Nina looked down at the forms on her desk and frowned. "You haven't been able to get a job in fourteen months?"

"Fourteen months in California," Elmo said, still carefully rolling his cigarette. "Six and a half years counting New York, North Carolina, and Florida."

"You're a musician?" Nina continued.

"That's right." Elmo's tongue wiggled as he licked the cigarette paper. "Very hard to get a job these days." He held up the cigarette, twirled it, inspected it, and then put it between his lips.

"How hard have you tried, Mr. Cole?"

Elmo lit up, inhaled, and leaned back. The tone of her question had been hard, but he was still softly smiling. "I go down to the musicians' union every week," he told her. "I read the papers, you know, the *Hollywood Reporter* . . . But you know, there's just no work."

Nina's eyes narrowed. "You don't have a current address listed here. Where do you live?"

Elmo blew out a huge smoke ring and speared it with his finger. "In my truck," he said.

"I see," Nina nodded.

"It's a good living quarters, my truck." And Elmo began to describe it as if it were a clipping from a *Better Trucks and Gardens* magazine. "I've got a Beauty-Rest mattress I picked me up from the Salvation Army. Not too soft, not

30

too hard. Firm. Just right. And I have my table. And a chair for visitors." He extended his hand as if he were graciously extending an invitation. "And I've got a book-shelf. With books in it. I even have an electric stove I can run off my battery for cooking."

"You're not married?" Nina continued checking down the form in front of her.

"No, ma'am," Elmo said. "No way."

"You have no children to support?"

Elmo laughed. "Not that I know of."

Nina noticed there were some questions he had neg-lected to answer. "Do you have any physical disabilities, Mr. Cole?"

"Well," Elmo traced his hand across his face, "it's kind of hard for me to get up in the morning." The hand re-vealed a self-satisfied, beaming smile.

This infuriated Nina. She thought of how she had spent the morning thus far, of how her clients spent most of their days. She had gone along with this over-aged hippie's little game long enough, she decided. Welfare was a real thing, a dire necessity for people who were in desperate straits, who could not get along without some help—even from the government. She knew that most welfare appli-cants only came to her office as a last resort, that few liked the idea of being on welfare at all. It was degrading to have to lay out the meaning of your life as so many answers to so many impersonal questions on a state-printed form; it was dehumanizing to have to go through all the red tape involved in finally getting assistance; it was nerve-racking to have to live in a state such as California, whose governor was always looking for ways to cut off any kind of help for the truly needy. And now there was this joker puffing away contentedly on his roll-me-down in front of her.

"I don't have time to play games, Mr. Cole," she snapped.

"I'm not playing games."

All right, she smoothed out his application form. She would give him chapter and verse, if that was the way he wanted it. "Mr. Cole," she began, "the State of California has to be very careful about who receives welfare. Not only because it has to be careful about the stewardship of the limited funds available. But also because it does not want to disburse funds to recipients who are unqualified to receive such aid for their own sakes. You see, if anyone receives—or tries to receive—welfare aid illegally, such a person is subject to a fine, imprisonment—or both."

Her nose stuffed up again, and she tried to clear it before continuing. "There are a lot of needy people, desperate people—"

Elmo interrupted. This time he was not smiling. "I'm needy, and I'm desperate," he said quietly.

Nina sighed. She picked up her ballpoint and jotted down her referral decision. "We're going to have to send a social worker out to your place of residence—I mean your truck, Mr. Cole," she explained.

"Sure." Elmo was smiling again beatifically. "When?" As if he couldn't wait to play the role of the gracious host.

Nina blew her nose. Her cold was getting worse as the day grew longer. Maybe she shouldn't have come in at all, she thought. Maybe she should go home early. Anyway, one thing certain, she wanted to get through with this joker. As a professional, sometimes it was very difficult not to get involved personally with clients, on occasions, but rarely had she so easily been turned off by someone as Elmo Cole. He was a man parading around as a boy, a case of emotional retardation. He was leading an unproductive life, obviously, and he wasn't even bugged by it. There was so much to do in this world, and yet he seemed content to do nothing.

"When you going to come to my truck?" she heard him asking.

"*I'm* not coming," she patiently explained. "As I said, it will be a social worker. But first there will be some more paper work to do on your case. And then we'll get in touch with you. How can we get in touch with you, Mr. Cole?"

Elmo shrugged. "No phone in my truck." He leaned over the side of the desk. "Guess I'll have to call you here. Can I call you here, ma'am?"

"Yes," Nina agreed. "Call me a week from today. By then I ought to know how things are progressing in terms

32

of your application." She stood up behind her desk to give him the cue to take his leave. But he wasn't moving at all; he wasn't ready to end the interview himself yet. "Do you have any other questions, Mr. Cole?"

"Matter of fact, I do." He rubbed his hands. "I was wondering if there was any chance I could pick up on some food stamps."

"When?" Nina asked.

"Right now." He leaned forward earnestly.

"Well . . ." Nina began. And she couldn't finish. Soon she was sneezing again uncontrollably. She grasped a handful of Kleenex from her desk drawer and turned her head away.

Elmo looked on sympathetically.

"Excuse me." She wiped her still quivering nostrils.

Elmo rose and searched through his pockets. He came up with a box made of Florentine leather, snapped it open, and extended it to her. "Try some?"

"What is it?"

"Try some," he repeated. "Good for what's ailing you."

It looked like half-baked grass to her. Shaking her head she asked again: "What is it?"

"Snuff." Elmo helped himself to his own remedy, pinching some into each nostril, inhaling deeply and then sneezing heartily into a long red handkerchief he produced from his back pocket. "Really opens you up, see. Dr. Cole's Magic Cold Elixir." He placed the box on the corner of her desk, as if it would be more tempting to her if it appeared to be uncontaminated by human hands.

Nina pushed it back toward him. "No, thanks."

"It's good stuff," Elmo said, picking the box up and assaying its contents as if for the first time. "Imported from London." He snapped the box shut, patted it, returned it to his pocket, and sat down. When he looked up he saw that Nina was riled; her eyes had narrowed, and her lips were pressed together tightly.

"Hey," he reached out, "whatsa matter?"

Nina swiveled back out of his range and bit off her words. "You seem to be able to afford some expensive little items, for a man who needs welfare, Mr. Cole."

Elmo smiled back quietly, his hands on his knees, his head slowly nodding. "I'll bet this job can bring you down, honey." He looked about the office cubicle and clicked disapprovingly. "Bad lighting. Bad venting. Bad vibes all around. And you have to listen to bad stories all day. But it's your gig, isn't it? You chose it, didn't you? So don't just lay it out on me, ma'am. I'm trying to make your day as nice as I'd like mine to be."

Something touched Nina that moment, but she would not admit it. Quickly she retreated behind her official pose and spoke in the diction of bureaucratic masking tape. "In order to qualify for food stamps, Mr. Cole, you'll have to prepare a listing of all your current assets."

"Nothing to it," said Elmo, "I can give it to you now. And you can take it down with a short pencil. I've got my truck, and I've got my instrument."

"What kind of instrument?" Nina wanted to know.

"Piano. I blow piano."

"You don't look like a piano-player." Nina suddenly smiled.

"You don't look like a Welfare Lady." Elmo smiled back.

"What about your current bank accounts, checking and saving?" Nina went on briskly.

Elmo laughed.

"Do you have any savings," Nina asked, "in any other form?"

"No, ma'am."

"Do you have any money at all?"

Elmo patted his pockets and began to remove a few crumpled bills which he piled before Nina.

She pushed it back to him. "How much do you have here?"

"I think I had forty-five dollars yesterday. So I'm a little lighter today. And I have some change." He deposited a handful on the desk. "Let's not forget my change."

Nina sneezed again, scattering his paper money to the floor. "Excuse me." She bent over to help him pick it up, and their eyes met. He was staring at her softly with an

34

unexpected tenderness. A smile escaped her, and he nodded as if he had expected it.

Nina arranged for Elmo to get a temporary allotment of food stamps and decided to go home after lunch. The cold was obviously getting to her.

4

I had a cold that day, too. I don't know who caught it from whom, but after all Nina and I were married and were sharing bed and bugs. Sniffling together at breakfast, we both thought it would be best to try and make it through the day at work and then have an early night of it. Nina left first in the VW—she had a longer ride than I in the morning—and I cleared the table, put the dishes in the washer, and poured a second cup of coffee and quietly contemplated the day that lay ahead for me in the office: it was nothing but a big pot of dissolving marriages.

Little did I realize that mine was ready for the same stew. Nina and I had our differences: she was more idealistic, she wanted a child more. But generally our values were basically the same, and we both genuinely enjoyed our lifestyle. We owned our house in Laurel Canyon. No palace, but a comfortable home for two. We didn't have a pool or a tennis court, but the garden was nice and the view was great. It was an easy house to take care of, and our furnishings were easy on the eye, too—a kind of mixture of Mexican and modern. Nothing lavish, but nothing tatty, either. We had a circle of friends whom we enjoyed and who enjoyed being with us. We'd go off for tennis weekends, trips to Mexico, and pilgrimages to Sacramento to protest Reagan budget cuts for the needy.

The best part of our lives, though, Nina's and mine, were our vacation trips to Europe. We tried to get over once a year together. And that morning I made a mental note that perhaps we ought to begin planning our next vacation, that maybe our colds were a little psychosomatic, caused by the worst bug of all—boredom.

I sneezed, cleared my nose, went out to the driveway, and gunned up my BMW. I love that car. Like any Angeleno, I'm hung on cars—the center of Los Angeles being, of course, the car you happen to be in at any given hour. And since you spend so many hours in it, you'd better like your own car, otherwise you leave yourself open for a great deal of self-hate. The car you drive is also a valid projection of your own image. To me a Porsche is too obvious, a Mercedes too stuffy, a Citroën too eccentric, a Volvo too unimaginative. I liked to think of myself as having a flair under my no-nonsense workaday office facade—just like a BMW.

My office is less than twenty minutes away. Still I roared down Laurel Canyon Boulevard, took Sunset over to La Cienega, and cut down Santa Monica Boulevard to Roxbury Drive. Our office is on the corner of Little Santa Monica, to the convenience of our Beverly Hills clientele. Most of them could walk over but, of course, no one ever walks in Beverly Hills. People jog occasionally, but that doesn't count. That's a matter of health, which couldn't possibly be attributed to a lack of wealth. Besides, no one has ever jogged to a divorce—except possibly me.

I parked in the lot beneath our building and took the elevator up to the top floor. Sharing the elevator with me was a red-headed Japanese secretary who worked for a firm on the seventh floor. She was stunning. We looked each other over and knew we'd like to make it with each other. Even if I had a cold. But all we did was nod a wistful "Good morning" to each other. So I started off that day with a pang—a sense of horniness lost.

But seeing Gloria helped, perked me up right away. Gloria was my secretary. She was black, and she was beautiful. She was everything a man could want in a secretary: a good typist, a good stenographer, and obviously a great fuck. Gloria and I had an *understanding*—we both dug each other physically, but we also knew that's where we ought to let matters rest.

"Good morning," I sneezed.

"Good morning," she sneezed back.

I wondered if I had caught the cold from her or had given it to her around the office. I didn't know whether to feel annoyed or guilty.

"Lots of colds going around now," I said.

"Seems to be the season." She wiped her nose.

"I'm going to have an early night tonight," I said.

"Don't blame you," she agreed.

"Think I'll watch the Lakers. They're at Chicago."

"Should be a good game." Gloria was a basketball fan like me. In fact, we met at a game at The Forum. And I was looking for a secretary at the time. Nina unfortunately never cared for basketball. Ask Nina who Gail Goodrich is, and she'll say something like: "Isn't she an actress in one of those TV series?"

Gloria pointed toward the door of my office. "Mrs. Cramer came in a little early. So I had her wait in your office."

"Good. And could you bring us some coffee, please?"

"Sure. It'll be ready in a minute."

I checked my jacket and tie to see if I looked properly sedate and subdued, sober and responsible. "How do I look?" I asked Gloria.

She put a sheet in her typewriter, rolled it into place, and then folded her arms and leaned across the keyboard. "Sexy," she said, and bit the air sharply with her teeth.

"Foul," I said, but smiled back appreciatively.

Mrs. Cramer raced into my arms tearfully. I patted her on the back comfortingly, reassuringly. "What he did to me," she began.

"I know," I said, leading her to the coffee table. Mrs. Cramer had once been a beautiful woman, and she still wasn't a bad-looking one. In her middle forties, she was well turned out and knew it. Her Jax slacks suit was black, and it fitted her nicely, contrasting vividly with her blond hair. Her eyes were red from weeping, and she kept rubbing them. "What should I do to him?" she asked.

Gloria came in bearing a silver tray with a pitcher of

38

coffee, cream, and sugar. "Excuse me," she said, and placed it on the table. "Shall I pour?"

"I'll take care of it. Thank you, Gloria."

"You're welcome." She smiled and walked slowly out of my office. She had a lovely walk, especially from the back, a kind of nonchalant litheness.

I sneezed.

"Gesundheit," said Mrs. Cramer and handed me one of her tissues.

"Thank you. What say we have some coffee and talk everything over reasonably and calmly, Mrs. Cramer?"

She sat down beside me. "I'm sorry I'm so upset."

"You have every right to be," I said, pouring the coffees. "Cream and sugar?"

"Black is fine." Mrs. Cramer patted her stomach. "I know I should control myself. I'm sorry I flip out so easily."

"You've been through a lot," I said, handing her the black coffee.

"Thank you." She touch-sipped the cup and pit it down. And then she began to cry again. "If we didn't have children, I wouldn't care. I'm not a selfish person. Or a puritan. And I realize not all marriages were made in heaven. But there are the children, and that's the major consideration as far as I'm concerned."

"How old are the children?" I asked.

She wiped her eyes. "Twenty-one and nineteen. But that isn't the point, either. You understand?" She looked at me imploringly.

"I understand," I said, "but what I need now are some facts, Mrs. Cramer. Does your husband know, for example, you're seeing a lawyer this morning?"

"My husband!" She spit it out as if any mention of him was too unpleasant for her to bear. "No, I don't think he knows I've come to see you today. No, I'm sure he couldn't possibly know I've come here today."

"What makes you so sure?"

Mrs. Cramer stood up and went to the window and looked out over the flatlands of Beverly Hills. Then she lifted her head and studied the Hollywood Hills and looked past them into the horizon. "My husband's in Peru," she said, as if it were part of the Valley.

"Is he on a business trip?" I asked.

"Business trip?!" she screamed, and turned around and laughed as if I had told the joke of the year. "Business trip! That's a good one, Mr. Blume. The girl is a stewardess for one of those cockamamie South American airlines."

"I see."

"I hope the plane crashes," she said bitterly. And started weeping all over again.

I went and put my arm around her. She leaned in against me. I could not help but feel her *zaftig* boobs heaving rhythmically against my chest. "I'm sorry I said that," she cried into my shoulder. "I don't want him to die."

"Of course not." I released her and blew my stuffy nose again.

"I want *her* to die," wailed Mrs. Cramer.

I had had enough. I saw I had to pace myself. Otherwise, I could never get through the day with my cold. I could give Mrs. Cramer some coffee and sympathy. But I couldn't let her extract my full day's supply of compassion. There were other clients, too, who would need me. "Perhaps we can pick up on this tomorrow. Or some other day later this week. Perhaps it'll be easier for you then," I suggested.

Suddenly Mrs. Cramer regained her composure. She sat down, took out her compact, wiped away some dripping mascara, took out her lipstick and dabbed it sharply, and moistened her little fingers and touched behind her ears with them. The operation took a matter of seconds, but she was a completely different woman by the time she finished it. Now she was all business. "Mr. Blume, exactly what do you want to know?"

"Just tell me what happened."

She breathed in deeply and let it all out in one burst. "It's very simple, Mr. Blume. My husband ran off with a cross-eyed airline stewardess from a cockamamie airline. Her name is Wanda Brophy. Common enough. But from

40

the photographs I've seen of her—and I *have* seen *some* photographs—she has an extraordinary body. As for her mind, I know nothing about it, but," she leaned forward confidentially and whispered, "I doubt if she has one. She looks like she goes through a dozen packs of bubble gum. A day."

I nodded slowly, professionally. "And what does your husband do for a living, Mrs. Cramer?"

"He's a doctor."

Dr. Cramer. The name sounded familiar. I knew I had heard it before, but I couldn't place it. "What kind of doctor is Dr. Cramer?"

Mrs. Cramer clapped her hands together and sneered bitterly, "He's a psychiatrist. And let me tell you something: he's going to need a lot of help when he comes back. A lot of help. Because I want the house and I want the Jaguar and I want the beach house and I want his complete retirement plan and I want a lot of money. An awful lot of money." She stopped. "Am I being a bitch?"

I shrugged judiciously. "Not necessarily."

She started crying again, and I showed her out of the office, telling her not to worry, that she'd be hearing from me, that everything would be taken care of. When I returned from the elevator I had another sneezing fit. The cold seemed to be spreading. I would be better off in bed. Or at least at home.

"How's your cold, Gloria?" I asked.

"Lukewarm."

"Mine's getting worse. I think I'm going to go home. Is there anybody scheduled that I have to see today?"

She shook her head. "There's nobody super-urgent."

"And God knows I have enough paperwork to catch up on."

She tapped the tray on her desk. "You sure do, boss," she said, giving her gravelly throated Rochester imitation.

"Now cut that out," I came back like Jack Benny.

I went in to see my partner Curt and told him how I was feeling. He all but chased me out of his office. "Don't come back here until you're germless. Go home and take a rest."

I packed my briefcase with the paperwork, Gloria helping me. Our hands touched. I clasped the briefcase shut. She was looking at me with her olive eyes; her titties were rubbing up against me.

"Foul," I said.

"Only technically," she replied.

Curt had said it wasn't necessary for me to work at home, that it would be better for me to just relax and let the paperwork lie there. And I should have listened to him. I know it may sound as if I'm kidding myself, but I actually intended to work—otherwise I would never have brought Gloria to my house. If I had planned to screw her, I could have just as easily driven us to a motel—or to Gloria's pad.

"You sure this is going to be the best place for us to work, boss?" Gloria asked as we pulled into my driveway.

I patted her on the knee. "It's the only place for us to work."

"It's a nice house," said Gloria, surveying the redwood exterior. "I'd like to live in a house like this someday." I turned the ignition off and looked over to see if she was joking, sending up a wisecrack. But she wasn't. She was simply being honest. There was nothing I could say except, "Thank you. Come on, I'll show you the inside."

Gloria stopped and inspected our little front garden, teeming with flowers, daffodils and daisies, tiger lilies and mums, geraniums and roses. "Do you take care of this?" she asked.

"Nina does," I said. "She's the nature girl who loves to grow things. I couldn't even plant a row of string beans."

I opened the door and led Gloria to the den, a little roomlet off our living room/dining room area. Gloria studied the Jasper Johns on the wall: it was a Geminini lithograph of one of his targets. "Do you like it?" I asked.

"No," Gloria said.

"It's art," I said. "Look at the bull's-eye."

"Bullshit," said Gloria.

I sat down on the sofa. "Nina doesn't like it, either."

"Then why did you buy it?" Gloria sat beside me.

"I didn't. It was given to me as a gift by a grateful client," I said. "And let's see if we can make some more clients grateful." I opened the briefcase and began leafing through it. Gloria took out her steno pad and crossed her long legs.

"Let's begin with Mr. Sendler. I want to write a letter to his lawyer reminding them not so gently that this is the second time Mr. Sendler's fallen behind on his alimony payments. And we don't like it. Check the files and use the same wording as the letter I sent to Russell when he fell behind."

Gloria is a good secretary, and in two hours we finished what would have taken us weeks in the office—what with all the interruptions and phone calls. And I began to feel pretty good—there's nothing as satisfying as having been productive when you expected to be absolutely zilch in output.

And the brandy we'd been drinking for medicinal purposes didn't hurt, either. There's no other way to explain why we did what we did. We were relaxing, work done, and I had already called the Yellow Cab people to send over a taxi to take Gloria back to the office so that she could pick up her wheels. I had also changed into my p.j.s and bathrobe, intending to nap away the rest of the afternoon with the satisfaction of having had a good day in spite of my cold.

We were talking about some of the clients, telling after-school—or out-of-office—stories about them. And when we came to Mrs. Cramer, Gloria began to do an imitation of Mrs. Cramer arriving at our office that morning. Gloria had Mrs. Cramer down perfectly, her alternate moods of sad loss and fierce revenge, her ambivalent desires to hurt her husband and get him back at the same time. And suddenly Gloria was in my arms carried away by her role, mock-crying on my shoulders like Mrs. Cramer. And then the play-acting stopped. We were holding each other for real, our tongues churning in each other's mouth, our hands exploring each other's body ravenously.

"This is insane," I whispered.

"I know," Gloria agreed breathlessly.

"You'll catch my cold," I warned her.

"I already have one," she reminded me.

We heard a car come into the driveway, and we separated. I could not imagine who it could be. Gloria shrugged. There was a ring at the doorbell. I went to the door and opened it. It was the Yellow Cab.

"Mr. Blume?"

"Yes."

"You called for a cab?"

"That's right."

I turned and looked back at Gloria. There was a trace of a pout on her lips; her eyes hinted of disappointment and profound loss. "I'm sorry, we won't be needing the cab just now after all. Change in plans," I fumbled. "Wait." I reached into my robe pocket, but of course there was no money there. I signaled Gloria. She found her purse, extracted a few bills, and handed them to me. "I'm sorry," I said, and gave the bills to the cab driver.

"I'm glad," he smiled. "Thank you. Have a nice day."

Gloria and I returned to the den. "Don't forget to put in for that money," I said.

"I'll take it out of petty cash. But do you know what you're doing, Stephen?" Her hand touched Nina's favorite chair, a cane rocker, and pushed it back and forth.

"No," I said. "Do you?"

"Oh, yes," she smiled.

"Well, then." I took her hand and led her upstairs to our bedroom. "What are we waiting for?"

It was something we both had been waiting for. For a long time. We both had known that we would inevitably make it together, that our avoidance had only been an extended form of foreplay. And now she was in my arms and in my bed, and neither of us was feeling the slightest tinge of remorse. Or surprise. Although I did not expect that she would be wearing white panties or that her pubic hair would be that soft or that her movements would be that dexterous.

I had stripped her slowly, one article of clothing at a time, unbuttoning her blouse, unbuckling her belt until her miniskirt fell to the floor. And then I undressed and we got into bed, our skins tingling against each other. I had never fucked a black girl before, and I told Gloria that.

"Don't worry, we have rhythm," she said, and sunk her teeth gently into my clavicle.

Still I wanted to study the contrast between our skins, her African black and my Venice beach tan. I couldn't help being delighted by it.

"Are you on the pill?" I asked.

"Have you had a vasectomy?" she replied, and went down beneath the covers as if to inspect for herself, rolling my cock about her mouth in sweeping swirls. I pulled her legs over my head and blew on her cunt and then gently began to suck it.

"You taste white," I said. "Vagina Vanilla."

"That's funny," she slurped, "you taste black. Cock Chocolate."

Soon she had me groaning joyously and her cunt was all but swallowing my tongue. We turned over and I slid into her and she held my face pressed down against her tits and I nibbled on her nipples while I pressed my prick up toward her clitoris and moved it in slow probing pumps. And now her long legs were wrapped tightly around me trying to push me in further than I could ever possibly go, and her hands had left my face and were clawing and clutching my ass as if that were the way to squeeze even more pleasure out of me. But then she began to come and it was not at all as I expected—a wild, primitive release. Instead, it was almost like a little girl, who was well trained and well mannered, her sounds quietly joyous, the gurgle-like contentment of a baby feeding, and she was showering me with grateful kisses. I stopped and held back while she grinded on beneath me pleasurably, and then I carried her long past where she had expected to go with long, piercing thrusts until she lost her baby cool and I knew we had reached that plateau of eternal mutual gratitude. And finally I came and she hugged me breathlessly.

"I'm a fool," she shivered.

"Don't say that."

"I am," she laughed. "If it was going to be that good with you, look what I've been missing. All these months."

"We weren't scheduled before."

She propped herself up on an elbow, dramatically black against the white sheets. "I have a lot of open days in my schedule now," she promised.

"We'll see," I said, and began to play again with her marvelous black boobies. I wondered how I could ever keep my hands off them again, refrain from calling her into my office and saying, "Lie down, Gloria, and please take a fuck." I could see many splendid breaks in the monotony of an office day in the near future.

Gloria's fingers were drumming on my lips. "Do you do this often?"

"Fuck?"

She tapped me. "No, silly. I mean screw around with other women. I mean women other than your wife."

"Sure," I said. "Before today is finished I have four more girlfriends I have to see: Za Za, La La, Lu Lu, and Rebecca. And I'm going to screw them all."

"No," Gloria insisted, "I'm serious."

"Seriously," I told her, "would you believe it? But this is the first time I've screwed around in six years of married life."

Gloria let out a low whistle. "Nina really must be something special."

"She is."

"I envy her," she said, and pressed me to her maternally.

"What about you, Gloria?" I asked.

"Do you mean do I screw around?"

"Yes," I nodded.

"What do you think?"

"I don't know," I replied honestly.

"Good," she laughed, and languidly reached for my prick.

Just then I heard a noise, an unmistakable noise, the sputter of Nina's VW pulling into our driveway. "Oh, my God!" I shot up in bed.

"What's the matter?"

"Nina!"

"Are you sure?" We were both out of bed, Gloria getting into her clothing, me getting into my p.j.s as quickly as we could. "It could be another cab," whispered Gloria. "Once a friend of mine called them and they kept sending Yellow Cabs every half-hour for three days. Like a computer going crazy."

"No." I was at the window looking down over the fence at the driveway. "It's not a Yellow Cab. It's Nina's yellow VW."

I watched Nina get out of the car and search her purse for our housekey. Meanwhile, Gloria was trying to make the bed and poke her foot into her shoe at the same time.

I heard the front door open.

"Should I hide in the closet?" whispered Gloria.

"No. Don't be silly."

"Jump from the window?"

I shook my head vehemently.

"This would be pretty funny," she whispered, "if it was happening to other people. Not us."

I could picture Nina downstairs, the mama bear, sensing something awry, walking about the kitchen, poking about the living room and den. Then I heard Nina sneeze. And somehow her sneeze released a sneeze that had been waiting within me.

"There's only one thing to do now," I said to Gloria.

"What?"

"Walk into the bear's den. I'll go first."

Gloria went to the mirror to do some last-minute primping. Just like a lady. I rubbed my chin. I did need a shave, my early-afternoon shadow, but I would not have thought of shaving in a thousand years.

I opened the bedroom door and walked to the head of the stairs.

"Hello," Nina called up. "Who's there?" I guess I had taken her by surprise; she was a bit frightened. But not half as much as I was. What do you say at a time like that? I said, "Hi." Then I blew my nose even though it was one of the few times that day it didn't need blowing. My brain was too occupied to pay any attention to any

47

signals sent from my nose; my brain was trying to think up a way of saving my whole being. "What are you doing home?" I asked feebly.

"My cold got worse, so I took the afternoon off."

"Crazy," I said. "Me, too." And I forced a sneeze.

Nina started toward the kitchen. "I'll put up some water and make us some tea."

Gloria came out of our bedroom. I don't know whether Nina could hear the footsteps or not, but I rushed into the breach. "I brought my work home with me, too," I said.

Nina stopped in her tracks and slowly looked up to the head of the stairs. Gloria was now standing beside me waving tentatively, "Hi, Mrs. Blume."

Nina knew how to add. She looked us over and put two together. She rushed up the stairs, sweeping past us, inspected the bedroom and slowly began to cry, the same way she had cried when she first saw the Piazza San Marco. Only this time her crying did not herald the beginning of something marvelous, but rather the end of it.

5

Nina kicked me out. No talk. No arguing. No let's-sit-down-and-try-and-be-reasonable sessions. Out. Just out. Six years thrown away because of one turn in bed. It was not as if I was screwing everything in sight; it was just that I had screwed once but it was in her sight. I didn't have to call a cab to take Gloria home, I took her home myself—and checked into the Chateau. With my brief-case in one hand and a hastily packed overnight in the other. And the next morning I was handling my own divorce. The fact that I also felt I had developed a case of pneumonia didn't help either. And naturally my partner, my senior partner Curt, wasn't the least bit sympathetic.

I like Curt. He tends to be a little bit straight, too much solid citizen and hard-working advocate. But his heart is always in the right place when it comes to liberal causes. I first met him when I was straight out of law school work-ing as a volunteer for civil liberties. This was a censorship case involving pornography; and if I had once visualized myself as a great freedom fighter, I saw that in the real world I might have to settle as a porn defender. My job was reading through "hot" books and underlining the "cool" parts, those rare passages that could be accused of having some sort of redeeming social value. Afterwords I would tabulate the percentages. This was kind of dis-couraging. I hadn't gone to law school for years to spend my time reading dirty books. But Curt, who was the chief defense lawyer, went out of his way to encourage me, pointing out that we were concerned with as legitimate a Bill of Rights defense as any other. "Naturally, I wouldn't want this trash in my house," he said of our client's publications. "But that doesn't mean I have a right to say you can't have this trash in your house. To each his trash is a fundamental constitutional right. Sure, I wish we were involved in the defense of something we could feel more righteous about, but moral righteousness has nothing to do with legal rights." And he won the case.

Afterwards, while I was still getting my bearings as a young lawyer, Curt and I would lunch together every month or so. And one day, after his partner died of a heart attack out in Malibu, Curt suggested that I join his firm as a junior partner. The firm, then as now, was mostly into divorce. And for a while I wondered if I would be selling out by signing on with Curt. Finally, I decided that divorce was every bit as legitimate as porn and joined the firm.

Curt has been good to me since. But not that morning when I was bereft of home and wife and should have been in bed with my incipient pneumonia. I was lying down on my office sofa wondering what terrible thing could happen to me next when he came in obviously upset and agitated and began to lecture me.

He paced up and down as if I were a jury trying my own case. "I am not here to bore you with my reaction and my opinion of what you've done."

"Good." I turned my head away and closed my eyes. I hadn't slept very well the night before, either. Perhaps I should have taken up Gloria's kind offer to spend the night at her pad; when you're feeling sorry for yourself it's best not to be alone. But instead I had tossed and turned all night, blaming the mattress, the elevator in the hotel hallway, and the traffic sounds from the Strip.

"Nevertheless," old Curt was continuing, "it would be dishonest of me if I didn't tell you how I feel."

I nodded. I knew what was coming. I said, "I see."

Curt sat down beside me like a doctor exhorting a sick patient. "I regard you, Stephen, as a friend, not just a junior partner. I think of you as I would a younger brother. Or a son," his voice cracked. "Both you and Nina have been like family to Karen and myself."

I nodded again. "I know."

Curt rose and went to the window. He took off his glasses and blew on them. "Karen is deeply distressed," he said with great anguish. "Deeply distressed."

"What about Nina? What did Nina say?"

He turned around and let me have it squarely. "Nina wants a divorce and she wants it now. It's a *fait accompli.*" Suddenly he was on top of me, pulling me up to a sitting position, shaking me by the shoulders angrily. "Why the hell did you do it? Only a fool goes to bed with his own secretary. Only a fool plays in his own backyard, so to speak."

"I didn't plan it, Curt," I said quietly.

"Nonsense!" he shot back, released his grip on me, and returned to the window overlooking Beverly Hills.

"Not consciously, anyway," I defended myself.

Now he came toward me as if I were a recalcitrant witness he was intent on cracking. "Do you expect me to believe you took Gloria home just to take dictation?"

I was sick of the kangaroo-court tactics. "I don't care what you believe," I flared.

Curt measured out his words distastefully. "You took her home to get laid."

I stood up and went to my desk. I opened and closed the drawers as if I were looking for something. But the only thing I was looking for was a way out. I laid it on the line. "Look, Curt. Do you want me to quit?"

He shook his head. "I'm just trying to understand you."

"Curt," I rose and went to him, "Curt, it was there, that's all. Wherever you look, it's there. In the elevator. In the supermarket. I've come near getting killed in the car just from looking at the teenyboppers. They stand there without brassieres, begging for it."

Curt mopped his brow. "It's very depressing. Very depressing."

My nose was stuffy again and my throat dry. I pressed the intercom on my desk. "Gloria, get me some hot tea, please."

Curt took the mention of her name as a cue. "About Gloria," he sighed, and his voice trailed off.

"What about Gloria?"

"She'll have to go, of course."

"Why, what did she do?"

Curt stared at me until I literally gave ground, retreating. "It's all so sick and messy and stupid," I said.

Curt shrugged. "It's known as divorce."

The door opened and Gloria was cool, I have to hand it to her. She walked into the office carrying the hot tea as if she were just fulfilling another request on another day on the job. She set the tray in front of me and our eyes met and she didn't give away a thing. She turned to Curt and asked him if he wanted anything.

Curt just swallowed and said almost sadly that he didn't need anything.

"Oh, Gloria," I stopped her as she was about to leave the office.

"Yes, Mr. Blume."

She hadn't called me Mr. Blume in weeks. I thought perhaps she was laying it on a little too thick. "Remind me to talk to you later."

She smiled, bowed to Curt, and left.

Curt shook his head. "We'll probably have trouble with the NAACP, but she has to go."

I held up my hand. "Let me handle it in my own way."

"Fine," Curt agreed. "But do it today, please."

I did it that night. I can't say I'm proud of how I did it, either. But there was no other way. I asked Gloria to have dinner with me. She agreed on one condition.

"What?"

"That I cook it."

"Fine," I said. "Where?"

"At my place. You shouldn't be running around town with your cold."

"I have a kitchenette at the hotel."

"I prefer cooking in my own kitchen."

"Maybe we ought to have dinner some other night?" I said.

"Nonsense," she insisted. "This is no night for you to dine alone."

52

So that's how we wound up at her apartment. I had asked her to dinner in the first place so that I could let her down gently with the bad news. Now I decided I would just have to wait for the opportune time. And somehow it just didn't seem to be presenting itself.

Gloria had a great pad in the Hills, a studio apartment with a view of L.A. below. She was in the kitchen making couscous and I was on the sofa, sipping white wine, digging the Otis Redding on the stereo. I shouldn't have been smoking with my cold, but I lit up a Gauloise, the only cigarette that could cut through my stuffy nose. I contemplated my future. If I was starting out life again as a bachelor, I certainly could be doing a lot worse.

But I did not want to be a bachelor. I had been a bachelor. It's a nice thing to be before you find someone you're sure you love. But I was sure I still loved Nina. No matter what she thought of me at the moment, Nina would get over it. In a few days she would see my redeeming social values again. One fuck! One lousy fuck—except that in this case it was a good fuck—couldn't possibly mean the end of everything we had.

The couscous was heavenly, even reaching through to my infected taste buds. In addition to all her other virtues, Gloria knew how to please my palate. So dinner was no time to break the news to Gloria.

After dinner we spoke of Morocco, where Gloria had learned to cook the couscous and had also picked up on some hash during her last vacation. We tried the hash together. Good stuff. Soon Gloria was doing a belly dance. You don't tell a secretary she's fired while you're high on hash and she's belly-dancing.

But the subject was always on my mind. Even while she relaxed in my arms on the sofa. Even while we pushed back the coffee table and converted the sofa into a sleeper. Even while we were under the covers, feeling each other familiarly now, kissing each other shamelessly, preparing to fuck away gloriously.

And even while we were fucking, pelvis to pelvis, downstroke matching upstroke, as smoothly as a couple

53

that had been making it for years together, I kept wondering when I'd break the news to her.

And afterwards in that pleasant satisfied afterglow, her head on my chest, her lips picking at the hairs, her tongue murmuring contentment, I decided I would have to do it now. I lit a cigarette and coughed out the smoke. "I shouldn't be smoking with this cold," I rasped.

Gloria sat up beside me and drew in on my cigarette. "You're not going to die," she said.

I pointed toward the kitchen. "Shouldn't we be doing the dishes?"

"They can wait until morning," Gloria assured me.

I thought of Nina and how she couldn't stand dishes in the sink overnight. Everything had to be put away before the next meal. Each girl was different. Night and day.

I turned to Gloria. "I'm sorry you had to be involved in all this."

"All what?"

"My marriage," I shrugged. "My divorce," I frowned.

"Don't worry," said Gloria, "I'm a big girl."

I looked at Gloria's naked body beside mine. Her round, caramel breasts; her flat, ripple-less stomach; her curving, rich thighs; her long, lithe legs. And I found myself thinking of Nina.

I shook my head. "I still feel married."

Gloria put her arm around me and kissed me softly. "You'll get used to it," she promised.

The words came hard to me. "I don't want to," I said. And I felt like a little boy who was about to cry.

Gloria's eyes narrowed. "She's a fool. If I was her, I would have scratched my eyes out. I would have fought for my man." And she hugged my head as if it were a trophy she was prepared to defend to the death.

It was now or never. She was going too far. "Gloria," I freed myself, "there's something I have to tell you."

She touched the slight roll on my stomach and laughed. "You're pregnant?"

"No." I took her hand and kissed it. "No. But Christ, this is tough."

54

"Say it," Gloria encouraged me. "I told you I'm a big girl."

I took in a big breath and counted to three. Then I let it out: "You're fired."

Gloria was livid, her fingers became talons. "You son-of-a-bitch!" she screamed. And tried to scratch my eyes out.

That ended my first day as a bachelor—unofficially. The official divorce came a few weeks later.

6

California couples can date their lives by their trips to Vegas. The time they saw Tony Bennett. Barbra Streisand. Elvis Presley. The time they hit the jackpot in the slot machine. Lost their shirts in blackjack. Broke even after an hour at the dice table. The time they went with the Bergs. Or the Fields. Or the Medavoys.

I didn't go to Vegas for pleasure this time. I went to lose what I treasured most: Nina. I don't know why she picked Vegas for the divorce, she could just as easily have picked Tijuana. Anyway, what did it matter? Are you supposed to revere the site of your divorce? Go there every anniversary and drop a silver dollar into a one-armed bandit in solemn tribute?

A divorce is something you want to make official and legal as simply and as quickly as possible. And when Curt told me it was arranged for Vegas—Nina wouldn't speak to me on the phone—I nodded and made the necessary flight reservations.

"How's Nina going up?" I asked, sort of hoping I might at least meet her on the plane.

"She's driving," Curt told me.

The flight to Vegas was depressing. It's terrible to be going to an exciting place without the least sense of anticipation. The airline served champagne, but that didn't help me any, either. Nothing could help me. I begrudged my fellow passengers their gaiety; I stared glumly at the smiling stewardesses. If I had been carrying a bag, I might have been taken for a hijacker.

At the airport I took a cab to the divorce lawyer's office. Parked in front of it was Nina's yellow VW convertible. I was glad to see the little bug. Almost as glad as I was to see Nina herself. But inside she treated me coldly, with that excessive politeness that is the cruelest form of human intercourse. We answered the questions, we signed the papers, we thanked the lawyer. How many times had I been on the other side of the desk without quite realizing that I was actually presiding at a private funeral? Nina was treating me—in a word—as if I were dead, as if I no longer existed.

I followed her out of the office into the bright desert sun, shielding my ghost eyes from the glare. Next door was a wedding chapel, a couple leaving it in awkward celebration, clutching a bouquet of roses. It was as if the slot vacated on the marriage rolls by Nina and me were already being filled.

Nina had noticed the newlyweds, too, but without any reaction that I could discern beneath her sunshades. And now she was getting into her car.

"Wait a second," I called out.

She folded her arms impatiently. "What do you want, Blume?"

"I just want to say goodbye." I held out my hand.

She ignored it.

"If you ever need anything . . ." I stumbled on.

"I don't need anything."

"I'm sorry," I said.

She looked me straight in the eye. "For who?" She got into the car, slammed the door, and drove away.

I thought about it in the cab back to the airport. I *was* sorry. Probably for myself. And I'm still sorry as I sit in Venice and write these words. Because that's love, too, isn't it? Sometimes being so godawful sorry, it hurts physically.

At the airport I ran into Arlene. I hadn't planned it that way. I would never have planned it that way. But it was like a cosmic signal had gone out. If my place on the marriage rolls was now taken, I had also been assigned a single's frequency. I had known Arlene and her husband —or rather her ex-husband—for a long time. I had always

57

been attracted to her physically, but since we were both allegedly happily married, why make a play for her? Then she got divorced, but I was still happily married. Now suddenly we were in the same ball park.

Arlene doesn't have the body of Nina—or Gloria, for that matter. But she is a giving person sexually, and her movements proclaim that fact. Her hair is dark, her face is oval, her boobs are ample, and her ass is regal, and in concert they all sing: Take me! She exudes an air of matter-of-fact, matronly sexuality, a kind of kitchen horniness. You almost know that nothing you can do can possibly surprise her, yet she has a few tricks that are liable to be new to you. And she'll perform them without any great hoopla, as casually as some women offer a second cup of coffee.

She spotted me first in the airport waiting area. I was getting ready to board a flight back to L.A., and she had just got off the same plane when she saw me.

"Stephen." I heard someone call my name.

It was Arlene. She was with a friend, a tall slim girl, named Dori Derfner, whom I had never met before.

"I didn't know you were a gambler," Arlene said, after the introductions were over.

"Nina and I came down here for a divorce."

"Whose?"

"Ours."

"My God!" Arlene was really shocked. She leaned against the life insurance machine. "When did this happen?"

"Today."

Arlene reached out and touched my hand. "I'm very sorry."

"So am I." I shrugged. Her hand still squeezed mine sympathetically. "I guess you're wondering what's happened?"

Arlene shook her head. "It's none of my business."

"You may as well hear it."

"Only if you want to tell me." She gave my hand another gentle squeeze. For some reason I did not want her to let go at all.

58

"Well," I insisted, "you're probably going to hear about it, anyway." I covered her hand protectively, and so now we were standing there in the middle of the airport, three layers of hands. Dori Derfner deferentially backed off, becoming interested in the newsstand.

"Nina found me," I began, as an airplane took off with a deafening roar, "in bed with another woman."

Arlene couldn't hear a word. "What?" she shouted over the sound of the plane.

"Let's have coffee," I said.

"Okay," she nodded.

"Better yet, a drink."

"Okay," she nodded again.

One drink led to another, Dori Derfner disappeared, and soon Arlene and I found ourselves renting a car, finding a motel, and getting into bed. Arlene's body was as accommodating as I had anticipated, and I was much more virile than I had expected. It didn't seem to matter which part of her body I would stroke or pet, it was as if every nerve ending she had was capable of producing an erogenous tingle. This general appreciation I found intensely stimulating—and emancipating. I could do anything I wanted as a lover, and it would be gratefully received. So there was none of the feel-each-other-out tentativeness the best of sex partners usually have the first time together. We made love as comfortably as if we were an old married couple, but with an easy detachment; this was sex for pure sex, with neither the memory nor the promise of love.

And I enjoyed Arlene's great accessibility—and excitability. I rubbed my cock between her generous tits, and she sighed delightedly. I placed my cock between her fleshy legs, and she squealed pleasurably. I fingered her moist rectum, and she gasped joyously. And when I finally entered her she welcomed me ecstatically, thrashing her hands about my head and back, her fingers finding my every orifice, while I teethed on her nipples and clutched on the pliable cheeks of her ass.

And when I began to come, pouring my liquid into her

own ready cunt, she was genuinely more concerned about pleasing me than gratifying herself. And I liked that, too.

Afterwards, we kissed our way back to quietude and lit each of our cigarettes affectionately.

"That was nice," I said as we began to compare notes. "I thought I'd be very depressed."

Arlene was as indecently cheerful as one of those women in the commercials talking about her discovery of a wash-day miracle. "When I left Saul," she purred, "I was depressed for three and a half years. A nice steady depression. Comfortable. I'd get up in the morning and wait for it to hit me. Some mornings it wasn't there and that *really* panicked me. But I found that if I waited long enough, I would get nice and depressed."

It depressed me hearing her say that, and I said so.

Arlene smiled. "I like Nina a lot."

"She's an extraordinary person," I said, and meant it.

"I think she's the only girl I know who really doesn't have any ego hangups," Arlene agreed.

I knew we shouldn't be talking about Nina, but I didn't want to talk about anything—or anybody—else. Maybe that was the real reason I went to bed with Arlene. Not to fuck her, but to talk about Nina. It was the only interest we really had in common. "Nina's very understanding. And very giving," I continued, not wanting to chance a change in subject. I knew I certainly did not want to talk about her ex-husband Saul.

But then Arlene suddenly became silent.

"What's the matter?" I asked.

"I'm thinking."

"About what?"

"Nina."

"Nina," I repeated, as if it were a mantra that would bring her back to me. "Nina."

Arlene sat up. "Are you sure Nina left you because of the girl . . . ?"

"Gloria," I supplied the name.

"Are you sure Nina left you just because of Gloria?"

"Of course," I said. "Why do you ask?"

"I don't know." Arlene pulled her black hair back into

60

a bundle and reached for a hairpin atop the Bible on the end table. "I'm just surprised, that's all. I thought you and Nina had a perfect marriage."

"We did," I nodded.

"Then I don't think she'd leave you just because of that," Arlene decided.

"Arlene," I said, *"that's* just why she left me."

She shook her head. "We used to talk about things like that at the Health Club. And I remember one day Nina and Helen—you know Helen?"

"Helen Martinson?"

"Right."

"I can't stand her," I said. "Helen Martinson may be a great gynecologist, but she depresses me."

"That's beside the point. Remember when her husband ran off with the hitchhiker?"

I smiled. "I handled the case. I got Helen a fantastic settlement."

"Well," Arlene's tongue flicked about her lips, moistening them, "I remember at the time Helen and Nina and I were in the Jacuzzi together one day. And naturally we were talking about the subject of marriages and divorces, our marriages and our divorces. And Helen said something about she would still be willing to take back her husband if he walked in the door. And I didn't believe her. From experience. I mean, I had had a chance to take Saul back after he had his fling, and I didn't. And we asked Nina what she would do in such a case, whether she would take you back. And she said that, of course, it depended upon the circumstances, but if there was no love involved in the affair you'd had, sure, she'd take you back. She didn't think she'd break up your marriage just because of pure sex."

"Nina said that?"

"Yes," said Arlene. "I distinctly recall the incident."

"Then I can't understand," I said glumly. "With Gloria it was pure sex. And our marriage did break up. Nina wouldn't take me back."

Magnanimous Arlene could see the light at the end of anybody's tunnel. "What would you have done," she asked like a Zen master, "if you found Nina in bed with a guy?"

"In two words?"

"Two words."

"Killed her," I said.

"There you go," Arlene nodded, as if she had just proved a great philosophical truth.

I retreated from my position. "I really don't know what I'd do."

"Nobody knows any more," Arlene agreed.

The whole discussion was getting to be too much for me. "I'm hungry." I clapped my hands. "How would you like a chili relleno?"

Arlene's voice went low and sultry. "Is that a new position?"

It wasn't. But we enjoyed some more old-fashioned fucking before ordering up the Mexican food.

7

Arlene was kind, gentle, affectionate, trustworthy, and a good lay. She helped me through a bad time. We enjoyed sex. But it wasn't love. Perhaps I could have kidded myself into thinking it was love if I had never known what love was. But I knew what love was. It was indelibly imprinted in the marrow of my bones, in the memory bank of my brain. I kept thinking of Nina. I kept hoping I would see her like a schoolboy with a crush. I kept dreaming of her as if she were someone who had gone away on a trip and would soon return. And when I could not conjure up her appearance in future fantasy I would will it into existence through memory. I would home in on moments we had shared, experiences we had treasured. I would retrace every minute we had spent together, as if there were a movie projector in my brain always ready to be fed with the spools marked NINA. And after a while I could stop the projector for instant replays and speed it up to get to the best parts. And I would never get tired of reruns of old favorites: NINA AND STEPHEN MEET, NINA AND STEPHEN MARRY, NINA AND STEPHEN IN ACAPULCO. It was weird, too. Because I began to lose control. I could be in court, conferring in chambers with a judge, when suddenly the reel NINA AND STEPHEN'S WEEKEND IN CARMEL would flash on my private screen: the ride up the coast, the fabulous house we rented, the continual roar of the surf, the long chilly morning in the warm bed. And the judge would be looking at me, regarding me strangely. Or I could be at The Forum watching the Lakers go against the Celtics, my eyes glued on Wilt, delighting in his deceptive Stepin Fetchit moves, when there would be a click, the crowd disappears, The Forum goes up in a mist of smoke, and NINA AND STEPHEN IN THE DESERT comes on. My real life subverted by my reel life. My present life an anthology of my past.

My favorite was always NINA AND STEPHEN MEET. Because that was the beginning; there couldn't possibly be the hint of an end in sight; there would never be a more rapturous time.

We met not far from our house—or what became our house—on a Sunday afternoon in late spring. Johnson was our President, Vietnam was just starting to heat up, and Cesar Chavez was our common concern. It was a fund-raising party in Laurel Canyon at a house near Mulholland for Chavez and his grape workers. The Beatles were still very much together, and it was their "Revolver" sound we were dancing to on an outdoor patio. I had noticed Nina from the moment I had arrived at the party, a California golden girl in white, sipping from a tall glass near the dollar-a-drink-please-contribute-to-the-grape-workers makeshift bar. Wordlessly I led her into the dance area, and she was a joy, responding to my every movement but with a comic fillip, making the funny, exaggerated gestures of a Raggedy Ann set to music.

The record ended, and "Hey, Mr. Tambourine Man" came on, but I was sweating; I hadn't realized how much energy we were expending. Yet Nina still looked cool, impeccably cool. I thought of Daisy in *The Great Gatsby* and almost immediately I was fatally transformed into a Fitzgerald hero: somebody who would eventually be prepared to do anything for the fulfillment of the romantic dream.

"I think I need a shower." I mopped my brow.

"I think I need a drink," Nina said, and started for the bar.

"I'm Stephen Blume," I got around to introducing myself.

She turned around and her nose crinkled in the sun. "I know."

64

We joined the crowd in front of the bar, looking for a line to get on. There was none. It was the usual liberal anarchy. "You know me?" I asked as we edged forward.

Nina identified herself. "I'm a friend of Bob Sarrison's."

Bob was a colleague of mine. We served on the same sort of legal aid committees. "Aha," I nodded, "I haven't seen Bob in a month. A couple of months."

"He's in Europe," Nina explained. "I got a card from him the other day."

I didn't care in the least. But I wanted to keep the conversation going. "Where in Europe?" I asked.

"Venice." Nina smiled.

I smiled back. "Lucky Bob."

"Yes."

"Lucky Bob in Venice," I repeated pointlessly, awkwardly. Fortunately, we had reached the bar. I didn't have to keep proving my brilliance as a conversationalist. "What'll you have?" I asked Nina. "What are you drinking?"

"Gin and tonic, please," Nina told the beleaguered amateur bartender.

"And I'll have Scotch on the rocks."

Again there was a beat of silence. But Nina saved it. She held out her hand. "By the way, I'm Nina Cashman."

I took it gratefully. "Hi." I did not want to let go of her hand. "Yeah, Bob Sarrison," I said. "Lucky Bob Sarrison. But did we two ever meet—you and I?"

She shook her head. "No. I saw you at tennis somewhere. You were playing, and Bob said he knew you."

There was a note of eagerness in my voice. "Did you ask him if he knew me?"

She shook her head and laughed. "No, I didn't ask him anything. He just said, 'That's Stephen Blume.' You were playing, that's all."

"Was he putting down my paranoia—I mean my backhand?"

"No," she laughed, while I paid for the drinks. Generously. Because she was watching.

"He should have," I said, handing Nina her gin and tonic, "I have a terrible backhand."

Nina sipped her drink and smiled over the rim of the tall glass. "I know."

I began to lead her away from the bar. "Have we been making banal conversation?" I asked.

"I think so," she agreed.

I looked around the patio at all the people. It was as if the party were suddenly divided into just two parts. Nina And Everybody Else. And I knew which part of the party was for me.

"Who do you know here?" I said, indicating Everybody Else.

"The Vickermans," Nina responded.

"Are you involved with the Delano thing?"

"Not enough. I should be doing more." Nina clicked her tongue against her teeth. "I give some money and I picket supermarkets. But that's not enough."

She made me feel a little ashamed of myself. It was more than I was doing. "Who are you with?"

Nina led me toward the living room and pointed. A baldish, bearded, hip-looking man in his forties was standing before the fireplace talking earnestly to a Mexican-American. "There he is," she said.

"The Chicano?"

"No, Jack Morrison."

"Is he your father?"

Nina laughed. "I told you my name is Cashman." I loved the way she corrected me; chastisement without a note of punishment.

I decided to level with her. "You're very attractive, and I'm desperately trying to be witty," I said.

"You're failing." She took my arm. "Want to dance?"

"Sure." I followed her back out to the patio. "But what about . . . uh . . . uh . . ." I gestured over my shoulder, "Jack?"

"He doesn't like these dances."

"Probably bad for his heart," I said, as we fell into the music.

Nina laughed again, her pearly teeth showing, her blue eyes sparkling. We danced all afternoon. We could have danced forever.

But the party began to thin out. Only a priest, some grape workers, and a few hippies seemed set to stay. But the great middle class was making the preparatory moves of departure. Women primping, men shaking hands, everyone thanking the host, a documentary film-maker and his young wife—or girlfriend. Car horns impatiently blared. The great evening event known as the dinner hour would soon be upon us.

"The party's over," I observed sadly.

"But it's been a ball," Nina said.

"Really?"

"Yes, really."

"Is Jack taking you home?"

"After dinner."

"Oh, you have dinner plans?"

"I think so."

I took her elbows. "Cancel them."

She shook her head. "I couldn't do that."

"Tell Jack you're not feeling well."

"But I'm feeling fine."

"Lie."

She looked at me with wide eyes. "Do you really want me to?"

"Sure."

"No," she decided, "but do you have a pencil?"

I handed her a pen. I found one of my own cards in my wallet, and she wrote her phone number on it.

"Where is that?"

"West Hollywood," and she added her address. It was an apartment.

"I hope your building has an elevator," I said.

"Why?"

"Too many steps aren't good for old Jack at his age."

"Oh." She mock-punched me. And headed toward Jack. Then she stopped, turned around, and waved.

The wave was more of a *hello* than a *goodbye*.

But I left the party, as I had come, by myself. Physically, anyway. I could not get Nina out of my head. I had dinner, I went to a movie, I came home and showered, I watched The Late Show. And Nina was always with me, her danc-

67

ing image a prism through which I saw everything and did everything else. I ate a taco—but I had to bite through Nina to get to it. I watched the movie on the screen—but I had to see through Nina in order to view it. I showered —but the water had to stream through Nina to reach me. It was weird, it was exciting; I was in love.

But what was I to do? I was bright, sophisticated, I knew I was supposed to cool it, that I ought not rush it. I was afraid to come on too strong but just lying in my bed, unable to sleep, smoking cigarette after cigarette, I felt immeasurably weak. I wondered if Nina was feeling the same crazy chemical reaction as I. Or was I just off on a solo fantasy trip? Hadn't she looked at me *that* way? Hadn't she sensed the lovely electricity? Hadn't there been *that* exquisite tension between us? Finally, emotion conquered discretion. I reached for the card and dialed her number. I was about to hang up as I waited for the ring, when I noticed the time: Two-thirty-eight.

But she came on the phone immediately. "Hello, Stephen."

"How did you know it was me?"

"How couldn't I know?"

"Then it's real?"

"I think so."

"Is there a gray mouse sort of gnawing away inside your chest?"

"No. But there seems to be a green grasshopper trapped there somewhere."

"Close enough."

"Do you want to see me now?"

"Yes."

"Shall I come right over?"

"No."

"Why?"

"It'll be nicer if we wait."

"It'll be torture."

"But nice torture."

"Then I'll see you for breakfast?"

"No."

"For lunch."

"No."

"For dinner."

"Yes."

"I'll pick you up."

"No. Let's meet somewhere."

"What kind of food do you like?"

"Anything."

"How about Indian food?"

"Except Indian."

We picked out a restaurant, we set the time. I did not sleep so much the rest of the night as float. I spent the next day enthralled, counting the minutes the way a child counts the days to Christmas. That night we met at the Chinese restaurant on Pico we had agreed on. It was closed. Monday night.

I couldn't have cared less. "I'm not hungry," I said.

"I'm starved," said Nina.

"I'll hunt a tiger for you."

"I don't like tiger."

"I'll hunt a lion."

"I don't like lion."

"I'll hunt a pastrami."

"I love pastrami."

"I love you." I wrapped my arms around her. We did not kiss. I just held her in my arms for a long time. We stood there in the empty doorway of the closed Chinese restaurant trying our bodies out for size with each other. They fitted perfectly.

"Let's not rush things," Nina whispered. "If anything is any good, it's worth waiting for."

"I just hope it doesn't spoil, though," I whispered back.

She fingered my lips lightly, then kissed me. "It won't spoil if we're careful."

"Let's always be careful," I said. And carefully kissed her back with all my heart and soul.

8

Within a month we were seeing each other every day. And every night. We were in love. Completely. We could not get enough of each other. We could not bear being separated. A friend of mine once said that if you locked a man and a woman in a room for twenty-four hours and they did not get on each other's nerves, then it was love. Nina and I could have endured eternity in the same room and called it paradise. We wanted no other world.

Her apartment was in West Hollywood, my pad in Westwood. Her apartment was bigger, mine was more convenient—for reaching both our offices. I had just started in with Curt, she was beginning her new job in County Welfare. So both of us more or less were living Angeleno lovers style—out of the trunks of our cars. We divided tasks fairly, automatically; I would cook as often as Nina did, she would shop as much as I did. I tried to lay out more money, since I was taking in more money, but Nina would have none of it. She insisted upon everything being scrupulously even.

Dutch, they called it, in those far-off new-nostalgia days of the mid-sixties. I guess it would all be tied into Women's Lib now. But Nina was her own liberated woman long before there was any such formal movement banner to line up behind. And though she had her problems as a woman —she had been into therapy and analysis—they never showed in the sexual arena.

Our sex life was a natural extension of our love—or literally a love life. We did not try to love each other because the sex was good; the sex was good because we loved each other. And it was so good we could even talk about it without ruining it.

I remember one weekend at my apartment. We had planned to go to Santa Barbara, but it began to rain. One of those unadvertised but intense and continual Southern California rains. Friday was obviously a washout; we would leave Saturday morning instead. But Saturday it rained all day, Sunday, too. And so we spent the weekend in bed making love, fucking—call it what you want—enjoying the most rapturous sex imaginable. If I would tire, Nina would spur me on. But usually I would require little encouragement. And progressively each sexual act yielded greater pleasure than the preceding one, as if there were a direct proportion between my constantly diminishing resources and the richness of the enticing rewards. But my resources were more plentiful than I had possibly imagined. I was as potent as a masturbatory teenager. I was able to keep up with Nina's insatiable female appetite. Almost, anyway.

Sunday morning, after two marvelous pre-breakfast fucks and a post-coffee one that was as fantastic a sensory experience as any I had ever had, I held Nina in my arms and panted, "That was, without question, the greatest sex I have ever had in my life."

Nina lay back against me, stretched her arms toward the cigarettes, and yawned proudly. "I'm incredible, aren't I?"

She put a cigarette in her mouth and then placed one between my lips. "You know what you're doing," I acknowledged.

She propped herself up on an elbow, lit her cigarette, then mine, and laughed. "But what are *we* going to do?"

"Move to a place where it really never rains."

"Seriously."

"Put me on a prison diet."

"No."

"Put you on a saltpeter diet?"

"No," Nina traced a finger along my face, "I mean it."

I exhaled solemnly. "I'm going to ask you to marry me. But first I have to ask you another question."

"What?"

I used my best cross-examining voice, the one I picked up from Raymond Burr, not the UCLA Law School. "Did you ever go to bed with Jack Morrison?" I asked.

Nina seemed hardly able to contain her laughter. It was as if I had just told her a big joke. "Yes," she said quickly.

"Oh, my God!" I held my chest as if I had been stabbed in the heart. And I mock-writhed with the pain.

"Any more questions?" Nina goaded me.

"Did you ever go to bed with Bob Sarrison? Lucky Bob Sarrison?"

Nina held up her index finger. "Once."

"Jesus Christ!" I shrieked.

"Never had him," Nina smartly shook her head.

"Are you a nymphomaniac?"

"Is that a question?"

I kissed her and we both laughed. "Maybe we should get married," I half-mused to myself.

"I think so," Nina said tentatively.

"Only *think?*"

"I don't know many people who *stay* married."

"Neither do I," I agreed, "but there seems to be only one way to find out."

"We could live together—really live together—for a while," Nina suggested.

"The trouble with living together," I pointed out, "is you're always thinking about when you're going to *stop* living together and get married and really *start* living together. Do you understand?"

"I think so. Even though I'm not sure I want to."

"I know what I want to do now."

"What?" Nina's hand moved down over my stomach.

"I want a big ice-cream sundae."

"Are you pregnant?"

"I'm hungry."

"Well, I'm horny." Nina's hand found my cock.

"Okay," I said. "First we'll fuck, and then I'll have an ice-cream sundae. Although I'm not sure it's so good for my health."

"Fucking?"

"No," I said, feeling my powers rise. "The ice-cream sundae."

We went to one of those ice-cream parlors in Westwood Village I hadn't been to since college, though I still lived in the neighborhood. You know: wire chairs, marble tables, old gaslight-like fixtures. And flavors featured on the wall that challenged the combined imaginations of Howard Johnson, Baskin and Robbins, and Clancy Muldoon. A tall teenager was behind the counter sculpting large scoops of boysenberry ripple into cones for the take-out people lined up before him. We sat at a table where we gave our "With Everything" orders of our chosen flavors to a little roly-poly waitress. Two tables over from us I noticed a middle-aged man slowly spooning a dish of ice cream while a seven- or eight-year-old girl beside him was eagerly sipping the dregs of an ice-cream soda. When the man saw that the girl had finished her soda, he pushed his still half-full dish of ice cream toward the girl and offered it to her.

"Do you see that?" I nudged Nina.

"The man and the girl at that table?"

"Don't stare at them. But tell me who you think they are."

"You mean, they're movie people?"

"No," I explained, "I mean what their relationship is."

"Kidnapper and kidnappee," said Nina.

"No, come on."

"A couple that met at Esalen."

"Seriously."

"Okay, father and daughter," Nina said. "What's the point?"

"Well, because of the nature of my work I don't just look at them and see a father and daughter. I see a whole scenario: A custody fight. A support suit. Haggling over visitation arrangements. So Sunday is the one day he can see her. And he's going to try to make the most of their day together. To store up enough affection in her to last until next week. He'll woo her with ice cream, he'll ply her with movies. But he himself really isn't used to kids any

73

more. You have to be around kids constantly to understand them. It's kind of sad and poignant."

The waitress deposited our sundaes, my guacamole-
peach and Nina's artichoke-melba. We started into them.

"What do you think they were like when they started
out?" Nina wondered.

"Who?"

"That man and his wife, the little girl's mother."

"I guess they were in love," I said. "Otherwise, they
wouldn't have married."

"Maybe they should have just lived together?" Nina
nodded her head wistfully. "They would have been better
off in the long run."

I reached over and helped myself to a taste of Nina's
artichoke ice cream. "Interesting," I observed, as I smacked
my lips.

I offered Nina a taste of my ice cream. She refused. "I
can't even finish what I have here."

I looked over at the man and his daughter; he was
wiping her face lovingly with a napkin. "In those days,"
I finally brought myself to the point Nina had raised, "I
don't think people lived together as much as we do now."

"Who have you lived with?"

The question somehow took me by surprise. "Does it
matter?"

"No," said Nina. "But I told you about Jack and Bob."

"You wouldn't know her anyway," I said. "Her name
was Miranda."

But Nina was curious. She wanted to know more. "When
was this?"

"My last year at law school. We lived together for almost
the whole year."

"What happened?" Nina pushed away her half-com-
pleted sundae and sipped some water. "How did it end?"

"Nothing really dramatic," I shrugged. "It just stopped
being interesting."

Nina leaned across the table. "There had to be something."

"Well," I fumbled, "she was an English major."

Nina laughed. "That's what ended it?"

74

I laughed along with her. "As much as anything else," I said. "Truthfully. The first few months it was pure sex. Miranda was the first woman I'd ever really lived with. Before that, there had been some women I'd spent a weekend with here, or a few days there. But never really lived with. So there was that pure sex to begin with."

"And after that?"

"After the sex," I thought back, "came more sex."

"Come on."

"Oh, we did a lot of things together. It was really very nice," I reminisced. "Miranda was very bright. And pretty, too. We both wanted to change the world. That sort of thing."

"Sounds like us," Nina smiled.

I finished my sundae. "I shouldn't eat so much sweet stuff." I took a drink of water and signaled the waitress for our check. "Listen, Nina, if you don't want to get married . . ." I said.

Nina snickered. She watched the visitation man and his daughter leaving the ice-cream parlor. Her eyes narrowed. "My parents hated each other," she said matter-of-factly. "And they were married for thirty-two years. It was terrible."

I reached over and took her hand. I could not help but notice again what lovely long fingers she had. How delicate they were. "My parents loved each other." I pried her fingers apart one by one and studied them. "They really got it on."

Her fingers danced away from me. "I don't want to be negative, Stephen. I just—" She clasped her hands together like a little girl obediently sitting at a desk in school, but there was a note of fervent adult prayer in her tone, and her voice became husky. "If we do it, I would like for it to last a long time."

"I would like for it to last forever," I said, and leaned across the table to kiss her. Then we both were silent in genuine awe of our love. "And if it doesn't last forever," I brought us back down to earth, "I know a great lawyer."

We both rose. "You're very sweet," Nina said.

I took her in my arms and caressed her. "And you're a teddy bear."

She growled and we walked out into the rain.

Westwood Village is one of the few walking areas in Los Angeles. You can saunter in and out of shops without getting in and out of your car. Usually, it is crowded with pedestrians. With UCLA students. With teenyboppers and groupies who like to think of it as their Greenwich Village. With moviegoers; screen for screen, it has more movie theatres than any other neighborhood in the film capital.

But like the rest of Los Angeles, it is allergic to rain. What are showers in other areas of the world are viewed as deluges in L.A. Cars skid out of control on freeways; people—never quick to take to the streets in the best of climes—abandon them completely. The city as a whole reverts to its aboriginal desert status. And nowhere is it more discernible than in Westwood Village.

Nina and I walked up Broxton Avenue back toward my pad, hugging each other, ready to sing in the rain, the sidewalks exclusively ours. As if we were the only passengers strolling out on the deck of a great ocean liner in the midst of a rough storm. Every few steps we would stop and kiss, huddling in the doorway of some closed shop. Before a bookstore Nina decided: "I want children."

I brushed the rain off her face. "Now?"

"No." Nina started walking again. "But soon. Very soon. I don't want to have my children when I'm too old to enjoy them."

"Is there anything else I can give you?"

Nina stopped. "Peace in our time," she said. "A better world."

"I'll work on it," I promised. "But what can I do now in the realm of the possible?"

"Just get me out of the rain," she snuggled against me, "and back into bed."

And we ran all the way home to my place, toweled each other dry, and got under the covers again with delicious goose-pimple shivers.

"Here we go again," I sang.

"Shut up," said Nina. And kissed me. But she did not stop at my mouth. She worked her way down and around my body until she had breathed revivifying life back into my rested cock.

"You are an incredible animal," I gasped pleasurably. "Go, go, go," I urged her on. While the rain beat ceaselessly against the windowpanes.

9

Rain spooks people. Here in Venice, especially. They say it gets too cold and depressing, too gray and despairing, too bleak and bizarre. But not for me. I like it here when it rains. The city is then in its natural element: water. I didn't come here for the sun, anyway. I was going crazy under the sun back in California. I *was* spooky there. So I don't mind the gray skies here at all. I fear the sunny days. Look what happened to Van Gogh under the hot sun.

I wasn't about to cut off an ear. But I was going crazy in my own way. And I didn't realize it for a while. Now I can trace my craziness back to the day it began, the day I was separated from Nina. From then on, it was as if I had some sort of middle-ear disturbance of the psyche. Nothing was ever in equilibrium again. The world was always tottering, and I sort of have had to lean to one side consciously in order to stand up straight. Things that I had taken for granted became an effort. Like getting up in the morning and genuinely looking forward to something that might happen later in the day. But nothing could happen later in the day that could possibly excite me, I would only try to recapture the remnant of the dream I had awakened with. My whole rhythm was shot, my life had to adjust to a new syncopated beat, but I was still moving to the same one the musicians of my soul had been playing before they put away their instruments and folded up their chairs. I've read about people who have had limbs amputated reaching months later to touch the absent member, even though the evidence of their eyes told them differently. I felt that way about Nina; she was a part of me even if she wasn't present. Arlene tried to make things easier for me.

She understood the balancing act I was going through. I didn't understand at all what was happening to me. I tried to make things easier for myself through self-deceit. I would purposely concentrate on all of Nina's worst foibles: the fact that she didn't like to sleep with the windows open, always required one more cover than I; that she never lied —a quality that is not easy to live with. I would picture her boiling her green plastic curlers in the kitchen, while wearing socks and my terry-cloth bathrobe, sipping sugary coffee. I would recall her utter embarrassment after being stopped by a highway patrolman for driving too slowly on the freeway. I would conjure up the remembrance of a tired Nina, conking out at a dinner party before the dessert and softly snoring. But then these images would all backfire. Overwhelmed by her vulnerability, I would pine for her more. Realizing how hard I had to strain to summon her bad points, I was inundated by her virtues. There was no way out.

Divorce is fine if you had a bad marriage, but if you've had a good marriage it's impossible. And Nina and I had had a good marriage up until our divorce. Which was both terrible and impossible. Such thoughts would swirl about my brain until, unable to find an island of sanity to land on, they finally came down on the other side: madness.

I became a visitor to my own life. My life was a visitor to me. We never traveled on the same ticket or on the same plane, like a couple that was afraid to fly together on the same flight. Every once in a while I would come in contact with myself, and it was as if I had run into a stranger. That's madness.

If I can date my madness from the day Nina and I separated, I can also date my awareness of my madness— which is the weirdest sensation of all—to a particular night on the Sunset Strip about two months after we separated. Arlene and I were filling the vacuums in each other's existence like medicinal pills made out of people. We would go places together, do things together, and screw together. Each of us was always there to give the other the essential fixes of human companionship.

I even began to think that perhaps I had matters somewhat under control—which was a madness in itself, the ultimate in self-deception. I brought Arlene to this super-hip health-food restaurant Nina and I sometimes snacked at. (You can't eat at a health-food restaurant.) What I loved about the place was the lure in the air of achieving satori by osmosis. Self-enlightenment hung over the joint like a smog. The waiters and the waitresses and most of the patrons all oozed with it.

We looked for a table in the outdoor section, fronting the boulevard, so we could get an occasional whiff of some cambon monoxide and sulfur dioxide chasers. I found one next to a bearded blond giant in boots and a long black-haired barefoot girl with a naked baby strapped to her back. She was feeding yogurt to the baby over her shoulders without even looking at the kid like Kareem Abdul taking a pivot shot. And she was hitting the baby's mouth pretty regularly, too.

"I like it here," I told Arlene as I pulled back her chair. "It makes me feel like I'm in the Tibet Forum."

Arlene stared about disconsolately. She was a girl built more for the Polo Lounge than people's parks, more for doing Tiger Rags than drinking Tiger's Milk. "I wish we could get a drink," she said.

"Order two carrot juices," I winked, "and I'll go out and buy some vodka."

The waiter, wearing a white tunic, and carrying a menu that looked as big as the original Ten Commandments, presented himself. "Hi." He made a peace sign, crossed himself and, placing his hands together, bowed as he handed us the menus.

"What's on the blue plate?" I asked.

He didn't bat an eyelash. "The special tonight is Asparagus Tips and Provolone."

"Domestic or imported?"

"The asparagus is organically home grown, and the provolone is, I believe, imported."

"Too bad," I said, "I like organic provolone. Meanwhile, we'll start with two carrot juices."

"Wait." Arlene signaled the waiter. "I don't want any."

"One carrot juice," I corrected myself.

80

"How would you like your carrot juice?"

"Squeezed."

"I mean small, medium, or large."

"Medium, I guess." Arlene was distracted. Her eyes looked past me, squinting into the distance. I snapped my fingers. "Arlene. Arlene."

"I don't know—" she began.

"Don't know what?"

"I'll order the juice and come back," the waiter said.

"Thank you." Then I turned around and looked where Arlene had been staring, toward the entrance alcove of the restaurant. Nina was standing there with a man who looked like Jesus Christ himself. Except a Christ who had been to North Africa. India. Mexico. The American West. And a few other places.

He took Nina's arm and they were walking toward us when Nina stopped in her tracks. She saw me, my head still poked around, and hesitated. I could lip-read Nina mouthing the words in shock: "It's Stephen." Or something to that effect. Because Jesus Christ sought me out and nodded something to her. She shook her head and turned to leave. But he said something, took Nina's arm, and began to lead her straight to our table, like a father taking a shy child to a new school.

I didn't know what I would do when they reached our table. I was shocked, paralyzed with jealousy. I hadn't seen Nina with a man I did not know for over six years. Somehow, since our separation I always pictured Nina alone. Fiercely alone. Independently alone. Defiantly alone. Perhaps even hopefully, abjectly alone. But always alone—never with anybody else. Least of all, another man. Especially a man so obviously in control.

I was wondering whether I should punch him in the midsection first and then get him in the face as he was bending down to cover himself, or to use a little *akido*: to bump my head against his nose, knee him in the groin, kick him in the ankle, sling him over my shoulder, and then get him in the face while he was trying to cover himself. I would show Nina who had more *cojones* in a hurry.

But he was standing over me, towering above me, before

81

my machismo could flare, calmly introducing himself as if he were the second coming of the waiter. "Hi. My name is Elmo."

Arlene waved. "Hi, Nina."

"Hello," Nina replied.

I waved to Nina, too. "Hi."

Nina said nothing. Looked away, instead.

Elmo put his hands on the table, leaned over, and stared me down to win my attention. "Let's just get past an uncomfortable place," he said calmly, "and sort of dig where we're at and know that it's okay to be in the same place and that sort of thing. This is a nice place to hang out, and you're here and we're here and let's groove on it. Okay?"

I did not know what to say. I was so stunned I simply nodded and said, "Okay."

Elmo's lips parted. He flashed some badly spaced teeth and rewarded me with a beatific smile. "Nothin' to it."

He took Nina's arm, and they swept by to another table. Arlene observed after them, "Did I ever say Nina was an old-fashioned girl?"

"Come on," I said, my face still livid with rage. "Let's get some old-fashioned martinis." As we stood, the waiter arrived with my medium carrot juice. I threw some bills on the table and pointed to Elmo and Nina. "Serve it to them. With my compliments," I said.

We went up the Strip to a meat-and-potatoes steak house. But while Arlene picked at her prime ribs, most of my nourishment was liquid. But I remained sober, stone-cold sober. And silent. My mind, though, was making all sorts of noises, asking all sorts of questions, and demanding a few answers. I was being immature, adolescent, unreasonable, I knew. But I could not accept my wife with another man. And she was still my wife, no matter what the law said. The law meant nothing. My life meant nothing. Without my wife. Without Nina. And I could even face up to the fact that my life meant nothing—after all, the lives of most people one encounters seem to exude all the vitality of a dead battery—if Nina's life didn't seem so fully charged, to be operating so efficiently. She was a woman who had a man who could steer her around rough corners. And that man wasn't me.

On the way home I almost steered us into a slow-moving Cadillac. Impatiently I gunned away from it. Arlene calmly exhaled from her cigarette and it was as if she were reading my mind. "You'll have to get used to things like Elmo."

I glared at her and turned back to the road.

"Talk to me, Stephen."

I said nothing.

"Okay," she resigned herself. "Don't talk to me."

What kind of heel was I, anyway? Taking it out on Arlene. "I'm jealous," I finally breathed out between my clenched teeth.

Arlene patted my arm. "It's normal."

I pushed her arm away. "Maybe."

Arlene flared. "What do you want me to do?"

I pulled up in front of my hotel apartment. "I'm sorry," I apologized.

"Oh, crap." Arlene put her head on my shoulder. "I should feel sorry for myself. Instead I feel sorry for you."

I kissed her. "I hope you're not in love with me."

Arlene dabbed at her eyes. "You're good in bed, and you feed my neurosis, but I'm not in love with you."

"You're a nice lady, Arlene," I said sincerely.

I parked the BMW—I at least had custody of that—and hopped out to open the door for Arlene. We picked up the key at the desk and took the elevator up to my room. I poured us two nightcaps, and we began to undress for bed.

I watched Arlene as she stripped. Somehow the process of Nina's undressing always seemed simple. As if in a pinch she could remove all her clothing with one magnificent gesture. Arlene's disrobing process seemed more elaborate. It wasn't as if she had all sorts of straps and buttons to undo. It was just that each article of clothing required a separate act, and the various acts somehow did not flow into each other. She removed her blouse and folded it. She took off her bra and placed it on top of the blouse on the dresser. She looked into the mirror and spotted something on her breast. She held the breast up to the mirror and inspected it. She sat down on the bed and pulled off her shoes. She stood up and unsnapped her skirt. She sat on the bed again, leaned back and peeled off her pantyhose. She gathered the hose, the skirt, and the shoes, and brought them to the dresser. She stared at her breast in the mirror again. She opened a drawer and removed the yellow negligee she kept there. And all the while she was talking. To me, allegedly.

"The first time I saw Saul with another woman I wanted to kill him. Literally. I was eating a tuna-fish sandwich on toasted whole wheat in a cafeteria, and I saw him walk in with some girl. He didn't see me. I picked up a fork and just squeezed it. Kept on squeezing it. It left a welt in my palm." She stopped. "Now I'm wondering if I'm coming down with a welt in my breast."

"What are you telling me all this for?" It was as if I could hear what Arlene was saying, see what she was doing, and realize that I was physically in the same room with her, but not handle all three inputs together. Each was joggling my brain along a separate track without synchronization.

I perceived Arlene nodding, as if she was getting to her point. "I saw Saul the other day, and I couldn't understand what all the fuss was about. There was this chubby little man with white hair and ridiculous sideburns and long thin cigars and a wife two feet taller than him and I said to myself: Is this the guy I was jealous about? And I laughed." She shrugged. "I don't think there's anything wrong with this breast, do you?"

"No," I said. "I'll be right back." Some emergency signal had flashed a message through to me with obvious implications that I wasn't quite ready to believe, that I had to check out immediately. If I had had dinner with Arlene and was now getting ready to go to bed with her, and Nina had had dinner with that hippie, was she now getting ready to go to bed with him? It was one thing for him to be Nina's man in public. It was another thing if he were Nina's man in private, too. It would simply be too much for me to bear.

I went into the bathroom, closed the door, and let the

water run noisily into the tub. I picked up the wall phone extension and dialed my old Laurel Canyon number.

On the second ring the receiver was picked up. I heard music in the background. I heard a male voice talking about "a heavy drug trip." And then the voice, the unmistakable deep, twangy voice, came on the phone. "Hello? . . . Hello? . . ."

I held my breath. I was afraid if I opened my mouth, out would pour vomit.

"Hey, friend," I heard Elmo, "is that a wrong number or are you a phone freak?"

I hung up and swallowed back my nausea. I had heard the truth, and it made me sick.

I left the bathroom. Arlene was in bed. Her negligee was on the night table. She was under the sheet, naked, waiting for me.

I put my hand to my head.

"What's the matter, Stephen?" Arlene sat up.

"Nothing."

"You look sick."

"No."

I pulled off my T-shirt and dropped my shorts and got into bed. I twisted around and turned off the light. I kissed Arlene perfunctorily.

Her foot poked against mine and then kicked it. "Aren't you going to take off your socks?"

I shrugged. She kissed me, squirming her soft tits against me, churning her cunt against my cock. I felt nothing.

"I think," I choked out a whisper, "I'm going to be impotent."

10

And I was impotent. Really impotent. Not simply a case of premature ejaculation. I just couldn't get it up. Arlene played with my prick in every way. But it wouldn't get hard. Finally, she gave up. "You're very tired," she said sleepily. "Let's go to bed." And she rolled over and slept.

I didn't sleep; I worried. I didn't like the idea of being impotent at all, not even for a moment, not even having known beforehand that I might be so. It was as if I had decided my cock was useless if somebody else's was servicing Nina. Which was ridiculous.

In her sleep Arlene turned over and groped toward me and found my cock. This time it responded, hardening pleasurably. I felt Arlene's cunt. Even in her sleep she was moist and waiting, ready to receive me warmly. I straddled her, preparing to make my grand entrance, my great comeback—and fizzled. The moment the tip of my prick touched the edge of her cunt, it squished down softly. I pushed hard, but it was no use. Arlene hugged me reassuringly and returned to her deep sleep.

I marveled at the way she could try to carry on a love life without disturbing her sleep. It was as if she controlled the depth of her slumber through some form of bio-feedback the way other people controlled their alpha waves. I despaired at how I could not control my sex life at all, allowing some undersea chunk of emotional iceberg to put it into a deep freeze. I had been impotent once before. But that was different. I had gone with a group of the boys from high school to Tijuana. We drank too much tequila and decided we would all prove ourselves men with whores. I wasn't that drunk, though. The whore I went with looked like she needed penicillin more than a penis. Still, I wasn't mature enough to tell her to just keep the money. I tried to fuck her anyway. And couldn't.

The next night when Arlene and I got into bed, neither of us mentioned the previous night's shambles. We went about the preliminaries as usual, as if nothing had ever before upset the script of our love play. And this time everything proceeded smoothly.

Until a few weeks later, when I was impotent again.

I immediately recalled the old adage that a man faces two crises in his lifetime: the first time he can't get it up twice, and the second time he can't get it up once. I called up Dr. Hearn.

Dr. Hearn is a psychiatrist who had seen me through some bad days. For example, unimportant as it may seem now, getting used to being a successful divorce lawyer wasn't easy for me to accept. I was miserable making money at what I was good at. I questioned the moral efficacy of what I was doing. I wondered if I shouldn't go back and be an idealistic starving lawyer again. Dr. Hearn helped me get my head together on these things by just getting me to pay attention to the glue contents of my own thoughts and desires. He didn't intrude, he just guided.

Dr. Hearn is a little man with a mashed-in face, as if he had run smack into a solid wall containing all of his patients' problems. When he listens he likes to play with a pencil, playing the tip of it across his lips. When he speaks, it's in a soft, high-pitched voice. But he rarely speaks; it's your money, your time, and he lets you have the floor.

"I thought I had it made," I told him at our first appointment, as I paused to light up another cigarette. I always chain-smoked through our sessions. "I thought I was finished. Oh, I know you're never really finished, and I know that life presents new problems all the time and I know I'm under a lot of real pressure . . . it's just—I don't know—I feel defeated. The thought of starting this in again with you is almost as depressing as losing Nina.

"I mean, I know she's lost to me. I know what she does

now is her business. But you should see the guy she's going with. Oh, what he looks like is his business. It's just seeing Nina with someone else that's weird, I guess.

"In any case, I'm here. I know there are no easy answers. I know I'm into a real, heavy dilemma." I also knew I was just making snowballs at the top of the iceberg and just diddling with them, tossing them playfully into the air, lobbing them from one hand to the other. And I could see by the way Dr. Hearn was playing with his pencil that he knew it, too. Finally, I decided to plunge right in and try to dive to the bottom of the troubling waters. "I mean, every time I see Nina with another man it makes me impotent. That's something real, isn't it?"

Dr. Hearn always answers a question with a question. "How many times has it happened?"

"Twice." I held up two fingers—the Peace sign that ironically indicated the extent of my inner turmoils. "Once the night I saw them at the health food restaurant and then phoned and realized they were living together. And the other time, which was two days ago, I just heard about them *being* together."

The pencil came to rest. Dr. Hearn tilted his head sidewards. There was a querulous expression on his face. It was his silent way of asking: Please amplify. What do you mean?

"I mean," I replied to his look, "Arlene—I'll tell you more about her later, but I'm sort of seeing a lot of her now—Arlene said she saw Nina with Elmo at a swap meet. You know, they have these swap meets on Sunday when people sort of swap things—antiques, heirlooms, junk. Anyway, Arlene just told me about it, casually mentioned it, and the next thing I knew, I couldn't have intercourse with her. I mean, I was impotent."

Dr. Hearn nodded. But he said nothing. Yielding the floor to the patient on the couch. Only he didn't use the couch with me. We always sat in chairs just rapping with each other—with me, of course, the rap*ee*. And I was quickly getting back into the rhythm of the analytic session, like a batter regaining his groove, a tennis player finding his stroke again, after a long layoff.

"Do you think impotence is just a symptom of something else?" I asked with mixed hopefulness and anxiety. "A symptom of something deeper? That it's just an ephemeral things that's telling me I'm guilty about that incident?"

Dr. Hearn pointed his pencil at me. "What incident?"

"With Gloria. She was my secretary. And Nina found me practically in bed with Gloria. Actually coming out of bed with Gloria. And that's why she left me and I took up with Arlene."

"Is Arlene the only woman you've gone to bed with since the divorce?"

What does that mean? I wondered. Why was Dr. Hearn asking me that question? "Yes," I nodded. "She's the only one." Then it hit me, what he was trying to suggest. "Oh," I snapped my fingers at the gestalt, "I see. Are you trying to tell me to go to bed with another woman?"

"I have heard sometimes after a man gets divorced he can go through a period of sports-fucking that can be very healthy."

"Are you telling me to fuck around?"

The doctor wagged his pencil. "I'm not telling you to do anything. You always have to tell yourself what to do."

On the way from his office to my office I picked up copies of the L.A. *Free Press* and the *Singles Register*. I pored over both of them. I thought of the time not so long ago when I was reading porno books for civil liberties and how far we'd advanced since then. Reality had usurped fantasy. You could now get what you wanted without reading about it. Or at least, so it seemed, according to the ads. First, there were those for products:

ELECTRIC SEXER

Amazing! Ecstatic! The ELECTRIC SEXER turns her on fast, fast, FAST! A streamlined two inch long vibrator capsule is connected to a small battery pack by a thin, strong power cord. Insert vibration capsule into vagina—hold in place with tampon—and flip the switch. Wow! Wild! Far out! Fills her with tingling erotic vibrations. Stimulates entire vagina and clitoris. She gets hot—FAST! Use during foreplay—or even before. Super turn-on for both of you. Tones up her vagina muscles for better sex, snugger fit. Comes in handy see-through case. Safe. Washable. Durable.

Maybe I should buy one for Arlene, I thought, until I got over my delicate condition. I turned the page. An ad that had a drawing of what seemed the face mask of a long-nosed, four-upside-down-nostriled visitor from a neighboring planet caught my eyes:

SUPER BAND SURGICAL SPLINT

The SUPER BAND SURGICAL SPLINT offers maximum support of the organ for almost its entire length. Two rows of finest spring steel bars permanently embedded in the bottom part of the aid, plus two extra bands, enables the patient to obtain sufficient rigidity for successful initial penetration even when the organ is in a limp or flaccid state. Removable elastic body for additional convenience. Comes with a 6 month lubricant supply.

Had I reached that stage? Would I need a crutch for my limp cock from now on? Other people obviously had come to that. Maybe the guy who had invented the Super Band Surgical Splint in the first place was someone who had suffered impotence as the result of his divorce. And his impotence was the necessity that mothered his invention. Perhaps someday I would view him as my heroic benefactor, the same way polio victims at Warm Springs once looked up to Franklin Delano Roosevelt.

I looked down the ad column. There were other ads directed at me:

ENCOURAGE YOUR PENIS WITH PETER ENERGY

PETER ENERGY is a 100% organic formula that actually helps resist nervous depression, guarantees larger and longer lasting erections every time. Rejuvenates sex. Overcomes impotence.

Was it a candy bar, a breakfast food, a pill? Perhaps I ought to send away for it. Better than playing around with messy gadgets. But perhaps it had a deleterious side effect —like causing your prick to enlarge sideways instead of forward in certain cases? At least, the gadgets couldn't cause internal damage.

I looked over the copy of an ad proclaiming AUTO SUCK:

Insert this vacuum suction device into your car cigarette lighter device and go for the joy ride of your life.

And what if your girl could have her battery-charged Electric Sexer working at the same time I marveled at the HIS and HER technological advances of our time, these marvelous labor-saving devices that freed our hands for more important things. But what more important things were there?

There was even a RUB-HER GIRL for those who could not find a real live girl. She was an inflatable doll that stood at 5′2″, had measurements of 37-23-36, "with soft realistic breasts," and it came with all sorts of options: Plain (No Vagina); DeLuxe (Penetrable Vagina); Super-DeLuxe (Extra-Soft Vagina with or without hair).

I could get a SUPER SPLINT, try it on RUB-HER GIRL, and then work my way up to people. Or I could try to make it with people right away. Forsaking the products ads, I whisked past the massage ads ("Coming my way," announced a nude girl, spreading her thighs, interrupting her orgasm to pose for the advertisement) to the classified.

I scanned them:

Get Laid! Tall over-sexed attract. stud, 25, will ball w dudes.

That wasn't my scene. I looked further down:

Weak, submissive man desired for encounter by strong, masterful woman who will know how to please you. Have best whip collection in Glendale area.

Nor was I quite that beat yet either.

Black Female desires sincere sex with stud any race who can get it on without hangups.

Could that be Gloria? Had I driven her to this? I looked at the address. It was a P.O. box, but not in her zone. Perhaps I should call this chick? But no, I was disqualified, I had one big hangup.

Finally, I found what I was looking for. A place where swingers congregated. After all, I was too shy to just call anyone on the phone, and I was too smart to ever put anything in writing. The particular place, The Alternative, advertised itself as a bar and night club for sexually free-thinking people. "Come in and have a drink, dance, and casually consider your sexual future. Many possibilities will certainly present themselves," the ad promised. But it also warned: "No dopers or freaks."

I drove out that night to The Alternative. It was in the Valley, and I was glad of that. I didn't want to run into any clients or colleagues. The décor of The Alternative was like any American bar, except that one immediately sensed a difference: the proportion of women to men was about the same. As I walked in, though, I was slightly embarrassed; I had never been to a place like this, and I didn't quite know what to do. Was I supposed to just sidle up to the bar and casually order a Scotch and Sex? Most of the people looked ordinary, as if they kept their swinging characteristics hidden for special occasions. The skirts on the women weren't exceptionally short, nor did their blouses reveal any extra cleavage. I started toward the bar, but before I could get there, a good-looking woman of about forty with a little too much makeup stopped me.

"Hi," she smiled. "You're new, aren't you?"

"Yes."

"I'm Shirl Terry," she introduced herself. "My husband and I always like to say hello to first-timers." And she sort of pushed her boobs in my face.

I wondered whether I was supposed to make a grab for one and fondle it socially. But I just said, "Great," and, leering at the boobs like Groucho Marx, managed to stammer out, "I'm Steve. Steve Babbit."

"Are you alone, Steve?" She poked her head behind me as if I might be hiding someone.

"All alone."

"Don't worry," she nudged me, "it won't be for long," and left me to squeeze my way into the already jammed bar. I noticed the reflection of a familiar face in the mirror behind the bar. It was my grieving blond client, Mrs. Cramer with the psychiatrist stewardess-prone husband. I wondered for a moment whether or not I shouldn't be his lawyer, rather than hers. I could get rid of Dr. Hearn and make a straight barter deal with Dr. Cramer: one post-analysis supportive therapy for one divorce. We probably could save each other a lot of money that way. But, I decided, in the long run we probably wouldn't be helping each other much, either.

Mrs. Cramer was making believe she didn't notice me. That was fine. I would make believe I didn't notice her. In that way nothing in our relationship would be upset. Anyway, we were more or less in the same boat, except that I had jumped into mine while she had been pushed into hers.

I signaled the bartender and caught his eye. He came over. "What's your pleasure?"

"Scotch on the rocks." I took out a cigarette and was fumbling for a match when suddenly a hand holding a lighter materialized before my eyes. The hand belonged to an attractive girl in her mid-twenties who immediately reminded me of a woman gym teacher. I think it was because of her nonchalant physicality. She seemed to be carrying her body most comfortably.

I thanked her for the light as I exhaled.

"Shirl said you were alone," she said, clicking the lighter shut.

"Right," I nodded.

She leaned into me. "I'm Cindy Chase."

"I'm Steve. Steve Babbit." The bartender put the Scotch down in front of me, and I picked it up and sipped.

"First time here?" Cindy wanted to know.

"Yeah," I admitted, as if I had somehow managed to misspend my entire life until my arrival there.

"I'm a regular," Cindy boasted.

"Do you want something to drink?" I offered.

"No." Cindy held up her hand as if I had mentioned some awful taboo. "Booze brings me down." She looked up at me hopefully. "Do you swing?"

I gulped down some of my drink. "I just got divorced," I tried to explain.

"Did you ever swing with your wife?"

"No."

Cindy smiled. "That's why you got divorced."

"So you don't drink?" I repeated.

"No," said Cindy.

"Then let's go ball," I suggested.

Cindy looked me over, her eyes settling on my crotch, and stuck out the tip of her tongue. "Groovy," she said.

She had her own car, so she followed me down Ventura to Cahuenga, then into Highland and over to Sunset to my hotel. The desk clerk was a little surprised to see me with someone other than Arlene, but I gave him my best man-of-the-world look. Upstairs in my apartment, though, I wasn't very much a man of anything. Cindy was all electrical energy futilely dispensed. No matter what she did, I could not get charged up, my prick clinging to detumescence like a baby to his rumpled security blanket. But it didn't upset Cindy at all. She got out of bed, still nude, and began rummaging through her oversized purse,

94

as if she might have in it some panacea—like a package of PETER ENERGY—for my ailing prick.

"I'm really sorry," I apologized. I was getting to be very good at making this apology, knowing how to time it for the opportune moment.

"Forget it," shrugged Cindy. "It's not at all unusual." It seemed my impotence couldn't have bothered her less. And I was grateful that she wasn't taking it personally. Why should my hangup drive others to the edge of despair? It was enough that it was driving me to that precipitous point.

"I'm still hung on my wife, I guess," I said, more as an explanation to myself than to her.

"Listen," Cindy was still picking through her purse, "before I started swinging I was completely screwed up sexually. Going to bed was like getting a tooth pulled. Our entire society is screwed up sexually. But one of these days everybody will be swinging and everybody will be happy."

"Swinging will solve everything?" I asked.

"Certainly," she intoned like any true believer. "What causes unhappiness? It's pent-up frustrations. In the sexual area. And these poison the person and poison the air."

"Do you think swinging will end the smog?"

Cindy didn't answer me. She had found what she was looking for—her address book. She quickly riffled through the pages, found the number she wanted, picked up the phone, and began dialing.

"Who are you calling?" I thought she might be calling some specialist. I already had a specialist, Dr. Hearn.

"A couple I know. Ed and Annie Goober. We can have a foursome."

"I don't know." I shook my head uncomfortably.

Cindy was all enthusiasm. "They have the best grass and the craziest sense of humor. Annie looks like Twiggy, but she's bigger upstairs. A sexy Twiggy. She'll freak you out. And I love to get it on with Ed. He's so free and easy."

"Wait." I put my hand over the phone. I guess I was still basically middle class, bourgeois, monogamous. Besides, I didn't understand the mathematical logic of the situation. If I couldn't make it with one chick, how was I supposed

95

to be able to make it with two chicks—and a stud? "Why don't we give it another try," I proposed, "just you and me?"

Cindy was amenable. She would have been amenable to any suggestion in regard to sex I had to offer. "Okay," she said, but jumped out of bed, went to the TV set, and snapped it on. "But let's do it with the television going."

"What channel did you put on?" I asked.

"Two," she said, putting out the light and getting under the sheets with me. Then she put her breast in my mouth and began to tickle my scrotum gently.

"Two is fine," I panted.

"Three times is better," she murmured.

"What?"

"I like a stud to come in me three times," she said. She bent over, reached for my prick, and teethed softly on it while she licked on it at the same time.

"Why three times?" my breath raced out of me.

"Because it's once more than twice," she replied briskly. Her cunt was above my head and I began to lick up at it, watching the TV screen while listening to Cindy moan.

It was the late news, and I was cured before they even got to the weather. Perhaps unknowingly Cindy and I had stumbled into a new kind of therapy? Or is that, in essence, what Masters and Johnson are all about?

The next Monday during my appointment hour I told Dr. Hearn of my great comeback.

"Hmmm." The pencil stopped. "What was on the news?"

All I could remember was the usual war stuff. Vietnam, Cambodia, Pakistan, Northern Ireland. "Do you think there's some significance?" I asked him. "I mean, some connection between war and sex?"

He seemed to think about it for a long time. But finally his answer was the usual question: "What do you think?"

11

All I knew was that I had made love three times in one night with a sexy swinger from the Valley, and I was more depressed than ever. My depression was caused by an obsession: I was obsessed with Nina and Elmo. I couldn't stand the thought of Nina being with another man. I couldn't stand the thought of what Nina must be doing with another man. I couldn't stand the thought of Nina being away from me. I couldn't stand being away from Nina. And I had to do something more than just talk to Dr. Hearn about it.

One night while I was at the Laker game, watching them play the Bullets, I decided what to do. It was halftime, and I had just bought a burrito and beer and was returning to my seat, when I chucked the food into the wastebasket and left The Forum. I got into my car on the deserted parking lot, turned on KFI on the radio so I could catch the rest of the game from Chick Hearn, and drove down Manchester past the San Diego Freeway to La Cienega. I took La Cienega all the way up to Sunset.

I knew where I was going, and I was nervous about it, yet I was in a hurry to get there. I wouldn't let a car stay in front of me on the road. I like driving on the highways built before the freeways. You earn your time on them, and you can make better time. I especially like La Cienega. Whenever I drive on La Cienega I think of Philip Marlowe. And that's an upper.

At Sunset Boulevard I turned, and soon I was racing up the Canyon. A VW camper was slowing me down. It had a bumper sticker reading: HONK IF YOU LOVE JESUS. And though it was a dangerous thing to do, I pulled out to pass it on a blind curve going uphill. I honked as I passed, and the bearded driver of the camper honked back angrily as he had to pull over to his side. "Up yours, Jack!" I shouted and swung around him. At the top of the curve was my old house where Nina still lived. I doused my headlights and parked.

Now I was really like Philip Marlowe. I held back the door as I got out of the car so it would make the least possible clunk when I closed it. And, ducking out of the line of sight, I sneaked around to the side of the house. Then with my back against the wall I edged toward the living room window. The lights were on and the drapes were up, and I could hear a jazz riff. I slowly raised myself to the level of the ledge and looked in the window.

Elmo was seated at a small piano producing the music. Nina was sitting on the rug, at his feet, eating a hamburger. The room was different than I remembered it. There was no new furniture I could detect, except for that piano, but somehow it all seemed warmer, homier, sloppier, more comfortable than when I had lived there. And the same applied to Nina. On the floor, eating the hamburger, digging Elmo, wearing an old Indian robe, her hair trailing down loosely, she seemed much more at ease than she had ever been with me.

Elmo finished his tune, took a swig out of a bottle of wine, and reached over to the ashtray for a skinny joint. He lit it and took a long hold-in drag. Meanwhile, Nina was looking up at him with lovely adoration in her eyes and applauding.

And peeping in at the window I started to cry shamelessly, tears cascading down my face, completely out of control.

I stayed up all night. I just drove around hoping to kill myself, doing everything reckless and dangerous and stupid that I could think of. I entered the Hollywood Freeway from an off ramp; I signaled left and turned right; I drove on the wrong side of Mulholland Drive. I went through Topanga Canyon going 70. But I had the luck of a drunkard. No car hit me. No highway patrol stopped me.

I finally pulled into an all-night diner in Santa Monica, took a pad of legal paper and an envelope out of my car, and drinking coffee into the gray morning, poured out my heart to Nina in a letter. Then I went out Ocean Avenue to Venice, to the parking lot of the County Welfare Office, and waited for Nina to get there.

I saw Nina's VW pull in, but she wasn't driving it. Elmo was at the wheel, Nina sitting beside him. Elmo parked the car in the open spot next to mine. I left my car and walked around in back to the yellow VW. Nina and Elmo were getting out of the car when they saw me. Nina's face turned white as if she had just seen a ghost. Elmo looked at me indifferently; he couldn't have cared less.

"What do you want?" Nina demanded angrily.

I felt like a summons server. "I wrote you a letter," I said, placing it in her hand.

"Why didn't you mail it?" She looked down at the letter distastefully, as if I had just placed a lump of shit in her hand.

"Read it," I implored.

"I don't want to read it!" she screamed, and tried to stick the letter back into my unwilling hand.

"Please," I begged again, a tremor in my voice.

Suddenly Elmo was standing between us. "Can she read it later?" he asked quietly.

I was in no mood for calmness. "I don't like you, mister!" I said threateningly into his face.

Elmo smiled back with all the friendliness in the world.

"Can't you see, he's crazy," Nina said to Elmo.

Elmo's eyes were still repositories of warmth. His mouth was curled in a gentle smile.

"I have to go to work." Nina glared past me. "I'll see you later," she buzzed Elmo on the cheek.

I would not let Nina pass me. I grabbed her arm. Elmo looked at me like a parent whose indulgence was being tested.

"Let go, Blume!" Nina spit out between her teeth.

I gripped her arm harder. I never wanted to let go of her again. I wanted to hold on to her forever.

"Easy now," said Elmo, and shoved me crashing into my own car. It didn't hurt me—just my vanity.

He came over to help me to my feet, but I waved him away. "You bastard!" I cried out.

Elmo laughed. But not so much as a taunt but as a rebuke, a chastisement to a child who was misbehaving.

Nina had no such concern in her expression or her voice. "I don't know what you want, Blume—" she began to say, her head peeking out from behind the protective presence of Elmo.

I cut her off. "What is this Blume shit?" I shouted back.

She ignored my question. "Elmo is very strong," she said, her eyes narrowing to the point of tears, "and I don't want to see you, and I don't want trouble. Please leave me alone."

My heart was breaking. I closed my eyes to hold in my own tears. "Read the fucking letter," I whispered urgently. And I extended the letter toward her again.

Again Elmo intervened. But this time, surprisingly, on my side. He looked at Nina and said in a voice of command, "Read it."

Nina took the letter from me, and he nodded approvingly. Then she quietly walked away into the building. The small crowd of onlookers that had gathered about us quickly dispersed as Elmo calmly but unmistakably stared them all away.

I was still shaking, though.

Elmo smiled down at me in gentle reprimand. "A lot of emotion can get you down. Leave you kind of weary."

I was as tired as I had ever been in my life. "I'm not weary," I lied.

Elmo laughed. "Well, I am. Got a cigarette?"

I automatically reached into my pocket, produced a crumpled pack, and handed it to him. When he returned it to me, I took a cigarette for myself. He lit us both. I rubbed my hand over my beard stubble.

"What do you do now?" asked Elmo. "Go to your office?"

I exhaled and shielded my eyes from the sun, burning its way through the morning haze. "Why do you ask?"

100

Elmo shrugged good-naturedly. "I don't know."

I turned the old Hearn trick on him. "What do *you* do now?"

Elmo smiled broadly, revealing a cleft in his teeth. "Go home and roll a joint," he said matter-of-factly.

"Are you in love with Nina?" I asked point-blank.

Elmo looked up at the sky, his eyes glinting in the sun, and addressed me as if I were a child or a fool: "What does that mean?"

"Do you love her?" I repeated.

"She makes me feel good. I make her feel good," replied Elmo. "Is that love?"

"Is Nina smoking a lot of grass?" I pressed on.

Elmo smiled again. "What's a lot?"

He seemed to know the old Doc Hearn trick, too. Had it down to a T. But I began to like him. Maybe I'm just a sucker for someone who answers a question with a question. Maybe it gives me reassurance, makes me feel I'm with a person who knows something—or, at least, knows enough to hide what he doesn't know. Interrogation is a shrewd mask, isn't it?

I called in sick, took the day off, and Elmo and I became friends. I drove back to my old house, and this time I walked in through the front door. Elmo handed me a joint. It was good grass. And pretty soon we were both high. Elmo wasn't very educated, but he was very bright, had lots of street smarts. He had been both down and up and knew his way around. And finally he had come to regard life as a game, a daily twenty-four-hour game, which one played with Red Queen *Alice in Wonderland* rules for the sake of the greatest possible amusement and the least possible discomfort.

We were in the living room, smoking up a storm, time appearing to slow down to a crawl, elusive truths seeming to peer out around corners to wink at us confidentially, as we compared our differing lifestyles. "I have to know what I'm doing when I get up in the morning," I explained to Elmo.

Elmo sucked in deeply. He had the lung capacity of a

101

deep-sea diver. "I always know what I'm doing when I get up," he exhaled contentedly. "I go to the bathroom, roll me a skinny, and have a cup of Yuban. Black with sugar."

"Why Yuban?" I asked.

"Because I don't like Folger's advertising," Elmo said.

I nodded solemnly. Under grass one doesn't so much understand things, but understand *past* things. Synapses are not only possible and necessary, but inevitable and pleasurable. The only problem is, you tend to forget the base from which the great leap forward was made.

"You're a total dropout, Elmo," I said with great admiration.

"Yeah," Elmo acknowledged, "but it's hard work."

And immediately, as if he had earned the right to food as a hard worker, he went to the kitchen, opened the fridge, and brought back a loaf of date-nut bread and a package of whipped cream cheese.

He put the food on the coffee table and handed me the joint. I inhaled deeply and handed it back to him, giggling. Suddenly it struck me as very funny being a guest in my own house smoking my host's grass. I could see that Elmo understood what I was laughing at—or, at least, I thought I did. I complimented him on the grass. "This is very good," I said, looking down at the joint fondly, like a man in a cigarette ad on the back of a magazine.

"Vietnam's Finest," said Elmo, as if that were the grass's brand name.

"I read they would give the boys a cash bonus to stay on for another term in Vietnam," I said, handing the joint back to Elmo for a last draw. "Then they would go out and buy grass with the bonus."

Elmo carefully put out the joint and then dropped it into a little wooden box. "I think I'll enlist," he sneaky smiled. Then he broke the loaf of bread in two and handed me half. I picked up a knife and smeared it with cream cheese. Suddenly I was ravenously hungry. So was Elmo. We proceeded to eat like gluttons, as if we had never seen food before. I looked at my watch. It was only an hour and a half since I had had breakfast.

"Were you ever in the army?" I asked Elmo.

"The army wouldn't take me." Elmo swallowed down his mouthful. He wiped his lips with his hand. "I got a record."

I don't know why I was surprised, but I was. Maybe I just couldn't picture a host in my own house as an ex-con. It was my turn to swallow down hard. "You were in jail?"

Elmo nodded slowly, as if he could still recall every day of it. "I spent a year inside."

"What for?"

Elmo laughed. "They found two joints in my car."

It always breaks me up when I hear these stories. But the lawyer in me insists on knowing more. "When was this?"

Elmo leaned back against the sofa and looked up at the oak two-by-fours in the ceiling as if the past was imprinted on them and he was just reading from one of many accounts. His voice was impersonal; there was not a trace of hurt or any other form of emotion in it. "Eight years ago. In Bayonne, New Jersey. A cop stopped me because my taillight was busted. I was coming home from a gig. The cop knew I was a musician, he could see by my trombone. So he searched the car—"

I objected reflexively. "That's illegal."

Elmo gave me that wise parent-to-child look of his. "Not in Bayonne," he shook his head. "So the fuzz found the grass, and they sent me up for a year. Me and my partner. Louis Herman. Louis blew drums."

"He was in the car, too?"

"Yeah."

"Was it bad in jail?" I began to ask, then stopped myself. "That's a stupid question. I withdraw it."

Elmo went into the kitchen, opened the fridge again, and said over his shoulder, "Louis killed himself in jail. Hung himself. Some stud raped him, and poor Louis never got over it."

"I'm sorry," I said.

Elmo closed the refrigerator and returned with a half-gallon of ice cream. "Want some?"

I nodded. He got two bowls, two spoons, and we polished the ice cream off. Then we lit up again and began to drink white wine. I could see exactly what Nina saw in Elmo, and I admired her taste. Elmo was like grass itself; he seemed to have achieved a point of humanity beyond what we usually call humanity. It was a heavy illusion, and he necessarily had to have a heavy habit to feed it and he had had to pay a heavy price to get there. But he still had got there with his own soul intact—which is something very few of us manage to do—and that came through loud and clear in his music. Elmo's sound was like the man himself, simple but containing subtle complexities, funky but drawn from a deep well of honesty; and it all seemed to be marked by an air of quiet control, no riff ever floating away carelessly.

Turned on, I listened to Elmo's music, and we drank more wine and got smashed together. It was the most enjoyable day I had spent since Nina left me, and I wished it would never end. But, of course, it had to. The time came for Elmo to pick Nina up at work. We tidied up the house in a way that made it only sloppier, moving messes from one room to another, laughing as we did so. Then we went out to the driveway, Elmo carrying a bottle of white wine. I started toward my car.

"Where you going, man?" Elmo wanted to know.

I pointed toward my car. "Home."

Elmo shook his head. "How can you go anywhere in that car and me go in this car and both of us share this bottle?"

In my alcoholic-pot haze I couldn't come up with an argument refuting his logic. I got into the VW convertible with him. And laughing, singing, smoking, drinking, we went to pick up Nina.

Nina was upset the moment she saw us seated in the car. A frown marred her face, and there was a nervous edge in her voice. "What is this? What the hell is happening here?"

Elmo smiled. "Hi, Nina."

"Hop in," I invited.

"Get out of my car, Blume," she measured out her words.

104

It struck me funny, and I laughed. "I paid for this car." And Elmo laughed, too.

But Nina didn't think it was funny at all. "You can both get out," she said to Elmo.

Elmo held up his hand like a traffic cop. "The man left his car in front of the house. Let me take him home."

Nina realized she had no choice in the situation. She went around to Elmo's side. "You're both schmucks," she said. "Let me drive."

We played musical chairs. Elmo squeezed over toward my seat. I tumbled into the back. And Nina took over the driver's seat and angrily started us away.

For a long time Elmo and I were cool. We didn't want to upset Nina any more. The silence was getting almost too heavy to bear, when Elmo took out a joint, lit it, and handed it to Nina. She took a puff. And it seemed to simmer her down. She gave the joint to Elmo, who dragged on it and passed it back to me. I inhaled quickly, leaned forward as close to Nina's shoulder as possible, and handed it back to Elmo. "If we get arrested, at least I know a good lawyer," I told him warmly.

He grinned back at me in appreciation. That gave me the courage to ask Nina my next question: "Did you read my letter?"

In reply Nina reached into her purse with one hand, extracted my letter, and held it up for me to snare, saying, "It's science-fiction. Completely unreal."

Elmo reached over and took the letter. "Can I read it?" he asked.

"Sure," I said.

He handed me the joint as if in equal exhange. I took a deep drag.

Nina kept her eyes riveted on the road and shook her head when I offered her the joint. I tapped Elmo to give it back to him. He looked up from his reading of the letter, nodding. "This is very beautiful," he said. And went on reading.

"Thank you." I took another drag on the joint and put it out between my fingers.

Nina was glaring at Elmo. "I want you to move out."

Elmo held up his traffic-cop hand. "Let me finish the letter."

"Tonight," demanded Nina.

"It's my fault," I interceded. "Don't take it out on Elmo."

Nina caught my eye in the rear-view mirror. "You're very sick, Blume," she accused.

I was annoyed. "There you go with that Blume again."

"If you're going to try to break up every relationship I have," Nina braked suddenly as the light turned red, "I'm going to get a court order. That's something you might be able to understand."

"I'm sorry," I apologized, realizing what I was putting Nina through. "I'm really sorry." But at the same time I wondered if she realized what she was putting me through. I just couldn't walk away from six years of love and marriage that casually. And she knew it. She knew me better than anyone else.

Elmo refolded the letter carefully, as if it were some priceless manuscript. He handed it back to me. "The man is in love," he said on my behalf to Nina.

She didn't take her eye off the road. "Why don't the two of you get married?" she replied sarcastically.

I could see what she was trying to do, and I didn't like it. She was going to take it out on Elmo for befriending me. I leaned forward and shouted into her ear, "I'll never bother you again! I promise."

"I hope so," she said quietly.

"But promise," I insisted, "you won't kick Elmo out."

Nina turned and looked at Elmo as if he was on trial. "We'll see."

"He's had a very hard life," I pleaded in his defense.

12

I didn't understand anything the same way any more. I still loved Nina, but I liked Elmo, too. Nina didn't love me; she didn't even like me. I was very confused; I was ambivalent about everything. I still saw Arlene—but it was just sex, a lot of fucking. She didn't seem to mind. And in one way I didn't mind, either. But in another way I did.

One afternoon I told Dr. Hearn about it as the tip of the pencil rested on his lips. "I feel like a wren, a slug," I tried to explain.

"What do you mean?"

"I mean I eat, I shit, I go to work, I screw Arlene. And I dream continually of Nina. Nothing feels real to me. I feel like I'm waiting for something to happen. What I'm waiting for to happen is for her to take me back . . ."

"Mmmmm," Dr. Hearn nodded.

"What's that 'Mmmmm'?" I asked.

"It's only a way of saying go on. Continue."

"You never said 'Mmmmm' before," I accused.

"I'm sure I've said 'Mmmmm.'" He wagged the pencil. "But perhaps you weren't listening."

"I always listen to what you say," I countered. "When you told me to try sports-fucking I immediately went at it."

"I never told you to do so in so many words."

"You hinted, Doctor," I insisted. "You hinted."

"You think I did?"

"Definitely."

"Mmm."

"Now that's more like it—your usual 'Mmm.' A three-M 'Mmm.' Not a five-M 'Mmm.'"

"Anyway," Dr. Hearn said, "you were saying that you were waiting for Nina to take you back."

"Only I don't think she'll ever take me back. That's the problem. Because I know I'll never be able to live without her. It's as simple as that. Look at me now. I seem to function, I still handle my work, but I'm always somewhere apart. I'm never really involved in it. Only one thing, one thought, involves me. Maybe I'm having a nervous breakdown." I paused. "Now don't ask me if I'm having a nervous breakdown. I'm asking you first. Am I having a nervous breakdown? I mean, according to your medical training and all your experience and observations, is that what I'm going through now—a nervous breakdown?"

"You're going through a difficult time, Stephen."

"Oh." I became hostile. "Is that what it's known as, 'difficult'? Is that what I'm paying you forty dollars a session for? I'll tell you something: I'm beginning to think this is a waste of time, too. What do you think of that?"

The pencil came to a dead rest. Dr. Hearn considered. "Perhaps."

"No, it isn't a waste of time," I countered. "I'm sorry. I shouldn't have said that."

"Where is the 'should' coming from?" Dr. Hearn gently reprimanded me.

Immediately I was abject, apologetic. Because that's how I was in those days. That was part of my craziness. My moods were mercurial; I would flash anger one moment and ooze warmth the next. No one ever knew what to expect from me. Including myself.

"I know there is no 'should,'" I said contritely. "But look at me, anyway. I'm smoking too much. Over two packs a day. I'm either missing meals or overstuffing myself at the table. I'm drinking too much. Maybe I'm trying to kill myself. I told you about the night I rode around trying to kill myself."

"Yes."

"But I've avoided seeing Elmo lately. At least that's a good sign. And I'm seeing you three times a week. Do you think I ought to see you more often?"

"I think three visits are sufficient at the present time."

108

"I mean, I don't care about the money, Doctor, I'm finding these sessions very helpful, now. I'm beginning to come along, don't you think?"

"Perhaps." He looked at his watch.

That was my signal. When his pencil went down and the watch came up.

I rose. "To be continued, Doc. See you Thursday."

Dr. Hearn stood up to show me out. "See you then." He allowed himself one of his rare smiles—or rather half-smiles. His lips parted just long enough to reveal his teeth and then clamped shut. And then he opened the door into his waiting room.

I walked out and stopped short. Nina was putting down a magazine and getting to her feet. We stared at each other, surprised.

"Hello," I said.

"Excuse me." Nina coolly tried to pass, but I blocked her way.

"Are you having problems?" I teased.

Dr. Hearn poked his head out the door and then came out of his office. He looked at both of us. His blank face wore an expression even more inscrutable than usual.

Nina pointed a finger at him. "I don't think you should have scheduled me right after him," she complained, shaking her head.

She had the doctor on the defensive. "You canceled your appointment for six," he said too quickly. "And this was the only other hour I had free."

"Mmmmm," I said.

"I'm sorry if I may have caused some embarrassment."

"I'm not embarrassed," I said.

The doctor ignored me. "Or if I may have caused you some pain," he said to Nina. "Let's discuss it."

"Good night," he said to me.

I watched Nina follow him into the office and the door shut after her. I walked out of the waiting room and down the hallway. I passed the offices of a skin specialist, a proctologist, a pediatrician, and then I suddenly stopped at the doorway of an ear specialist. I turned around and walked back to Dr. Hearn's office. The waiting-room door

109

was open, as I had left it. I tiptoed into the waiting room and super-quietly edged my way to the office door. I pressed my ear up against the door. All I could hear were murmurs, faint sounds, nothing distinguishable. But when I cupped my hand over my ear I was able to clearly make out Nina's voice.

"Sexually, I feel just fine," she was telling Dr. Hearn. "We had a little trouble at first, but I think it was because I went off the pill. It was making me nauseous occasionally, and I was beginning to worry about everything deleterious I'd read about them. But it was difficult getting used to a diaphragm . . ."

That was all tough stuff for me to hear. But pretty soon it got worse. She began to talk about her sex life with Elmo. I strained to listen.

"Our relationship is okay. I like him. Elmo. I always call him *him,* don't I? He's very kind . . . Oh, I know it won't last, though, but I don't know . . ." Her voice trailed off.

I could visualize Hearn sitting there, the pencil on his lips, patiently waiting for her to start talking again.

"I just wonder what I'm doing, you know," she said quietly.

"Mmmmm," I overheard Hearn. So Nina was the patient who got the five-M 'Mmmmm's. Maybe that's how he rated his patients. The more he liked the patient, the more 'M's he got. Nina was a five-M-er. I was only a three-M-er. And there were some poor slobs who only got a one-M 'M.' Or maybe it was the other way around? The sicker you were, the more 'M's you got. And Nina was worse off than me. When you got eight 'M's—'Mmmmmmmm,' for example—it meant you were close to being put away. And perhaps that's how psychiatrists shop-talked: "I saw four six-M-ers and one three-M-er today, but it was a lousy two-M-er who really gave me a hard time.'

"Mmmmm, and how do you feel about your ex-husband?"

"I feel better about Blume; that's really over. But I

would still like to get over the anger I feel whenever I see him."

"Mmmmm," said Dr. Hearn. "You're entitled to feel sorry."

I became angry. The nerve of that son-of-a-bitch. Whose side was he on, anyway? I made a mental resolution to cut back on my appointment schedule with him. Who needed him? It was a waste of time. Here it was just fifteen minutes after my session and I was feeling more depressed than ever. And it was because of him.

My ears perked up; my thoughts were obliterated. "Maybe I'm paranoid, Dr. Hearn," I heard Nina saying, "but I have the feeling that Blume is listening."

There was a long silence. I could picture Hearn's pencil suddenly stationary, a pendulum rendered immobile as time stopped.

"I'm sorry," Nina continued, "I just feel he's listening. Something just tells me he's listening."

"Do you want," I heard a scuffling of chairs, "to open the door and see?"

I backed away from the door on tiptoe in double time. I ran down the hallway, still on tiptoe, until I swung around the corner to the stairway exit. Still on tiptoe I hopped down the stairs to the street. I tiptoed into my car and made my getaway, wondering if Philip Marlowe had ever studied ballet dancing before becoming a private eye.

13

Knowing that Nina was miserable made me feel very good—for about a day. Then I began to feel more miserable than ever; I realized that I was responsible for the misery of two people. And contrary to popular belief, misery doesn't always like company—especially when the company is provided by the person you love. And I was in love with Nina to the point of physical pain. I was so in love with Nina that I became even crazier, and I took it out on poor Arlene. So that made three people I was making miserable.

One night after Arlene and I had made love, I felt I had to start doing something to resolve it. "I'm sorry, Arlene," I said.

Arlene was so miserable she didn't even know she was miserable. "For what?" She cuddled in against me, her hand idly straying down to my prick again. "That was terrific."

"I don't feel I'm being honest with you," I leveled. "I like you. I really do. And I know we've got an understanding."

Her hand found my prick, and she caressed it gently. Her shoulders shook slightly. "You're in love with Nina." She smiled, not troubled at all.

"Right." My prick was hardening.

"I know. I told you," said Arlene. She pushed off the top sheet and slid down to the foot of the bed. "It doesn't bother me," she said, and slowly put my prick between her lips and began to rock up and down, her tongue swirling gently about within her mouth, caressing the tip of my prick.

"Does it bother you," I panted, "that I'm *using* you?"

"Does it bother you," she slurped back pleasurably, "that I'm using *you?*"

I looked up at the ceiling, at the shadows cast there by the swirling drapes and Arlene's bobbing head. "It's not the same thing," I moaned. And I decided to let her have it. The whole truth. For her sake. "You don't think of Saul when we make love."

Arlene's head jerked up, ejecting my prick, just as I was about to come. "You're making me nauseated."

My moaning turned from one of pleasure to that of pain. "I think of Nina when we make love," I admitted, feeling nausea myself.

"All the time?"

"No," I writhed, "not all the time."

Arlene seemed slightly relieved. "I have other thoughts going through my mind sometimes," she admitted.

"But most of the time," I blurted out in spite of myself, "I do think of Nina."

Arlene was stung. Her eyes narrowed. "What about just now?" she asked.

"Yes." I shook my head and heaved my shoulders.

"What about before?"

"Yes."

"The whole time?"

I had hurt her. I did not want to hurt her more. There was no point to it. It was not for me to choose her form of misery. "Part of the time," I lied.

But she had received the brunt of my message. She fell silently on the bed beside me and began to weep, sobbing into the pillow. I reached over to touch her. She wailed louder. "I'm sorry, Arlene." I massaged her quivering shoulders. "I'm crazy, I guess."

She continued to weep, and I continued to apologize. "I'm obsessed, you know that. I don't know what the hell to do. But I don't want to hurt you. And I thought not letting someone know the truth is the ultimate hurt you can inflict on them."

Arlene stopped sniffling, reached over to the end table

113

for a handful of Kleenex, and blew her nose. "You know why I'm crying?" she asked, dabbing at her nostrils.

"Yeah," I nodded sympathetically.

"No, you don't." Arlene shook her head and began to cry all over again. "I'm crying because in spite of everything you just told me, I'm willing to go on the same way." She wiped her eyes and blew her nose all over again. "What a terrible thing to know about yourself."

Suddenly she flung her naked body around me. "In spite of the fact that you told me you see Nina when we make love," she rubbed her tits against me until I could feel the nipples hardening, "I'm willing, *willing* to go on. I want to go on."

The confession of our abject states perversely made us both more erotic. Besides, there was unfinished business to attend to. I kissed Arlene on the cheek. She took my face into her hands, and we kissed on the lips and then more deeply. I sucked on her nipple, and soon she had my cock in her mouth again.

"I promise," my finger found the entrance to her ass, "I won't see her this time."

"Who?" Arlene's hand squeezed my prick as if it were the neck of a turkey on Thanksgiving morning. Then she sat down on it, her back to me, hunched on her knees, grinding away, my hands reaching up and around to clutch her tits, until I turned her around and over, for the last sharp shrieking thrusts home, thinking all the while of Nina.

Afterwards, of course, I lied to Arlene. I couldn't have gone through that scene again. Yet I've never had respect for men who used women. I could never understand how a man could find pleasure if the woman didn't. On the one hand, maybe I wasn't really using Arlene. But on the other hand, who was I kidding? Being with one woman and constantly thinking of another is using. There is no escaping it. I thought of Nina. But then I am always thinking of Nina. I think of Nina now as I write these words in my room in the Hotel Danielli in Venice.

It is a pleasant room in a pleasant hotel on a pleasant day in a beautiful city. The shades are up this morning,

114

and the sun is shining. I see the boats in the canal. I have spent the week sightseeing again, waiting, and mostly remembering on these pages. And now as I look out the window and see a black gondola, the gondolier standing and rowing, a couple cuddled up at the other end, I recall the last time Nina and I came to Venice together. That was three years ago on our second honeymoon: I guess I still thought of marriage as an attempt at extended honeymooning. I realize now that perhaps we had problems that I refused to recognize, that I chose to ignore rather than attempt to resolve. And that Nina felt the pangs of these problems much more keenly than I.

One of the chief problems was the fact that we had no children. At first we didn't want any. We were just too busy getting used to the joys and routines of marriage. Naturally, then, of course Nina got pregnant. It was during our fourth month of marriage. We weren't quite prepared for the idea, but we were happy to accept it. I began to anticipate fatherhood: taking my kid to Laker games; helping him set up his first set of electric trains; going camping with him. And Nina was the same way. We played naming games and profession games and what-would-he-look-like games. We'd scramble our features into the worst combination and shudder; or we'd assign him the best of each of us and marvel at his beauty. But the kid never came. The pregnancy didn't work out. And from the start there were clues: Nina had show—or stain—after a month and a half. She was often in pain, and the slight bleeding would rarely stop. The doctor told her to quit her job, but she was too involved to do that. She was supposed to rest on weekends, too, but I wouldn't let her do that; I was so proud of my new wife, I wanted to take her everywhere, to be seen by everyone with her. And somehow the process of childbearing did not seem so complicated to me, so beset with pitfalls. I had only known it from a distance. I would hear of someone being pregnant one day, and then another day I would be informed of the birth of the baby. And I would never quite visualize the arduous journey in between. But during Nina's pregnancy I watched the agony and the pain and the suffering. And the worst experience of all: the futility.

On a Saturday afternoon just after the third month, we came home from an afternoon of art gallery browsing on La Cienega. Nina went into the kitchen to prepare dinner. And soon I heard a low moan. I rushed in to find her sitting down, holding her lower abdomen, beads of perspiration on her brow.

"What's the matter, honey?" I rubbed her back.

"I don't know," she said, "I just went to the bathroom and there was a lot of bleeding and then he began to hurt."

I called the obstetrician but, of course, all I got was the answering service. I left our number. I helped Nina into the living room so she could lie down on the sofa. Then I called my partner Curt. He put his wife Karen on. She said it sounded like a miscarriage to her.

When I hung up, the phone rang again instantly. It was our obstetrician. He asked about the pain: was it constant? Nina nodded from the sofa that it was. He said that he would call the hospital and make arrangements for Nina's admittance and call back in five minutes, but that meanwhile I was to get Nina ready.

I went upstairs and threw some toilet articles and a negligee and some underwear into an overnight bag. As I was stuffing it in, the phone rang again. The doctor said he would meet us at the hospital in twenty minutes, that they were expecting us.

I helped Nina into the car, kissing her every step of the way, assuring her of how much I would always love her, wishing with all my heart that I could be bearing the pain instead of her, hoping that the experience would not traumatize her. I raced down the Canyon, turned left on Fountain and got to the hospital, the Cedars of Lebanon, in less than fifteen minutes, having to stop for only one light on the way.

The admitting desk was expecting us, the clerk called the maternity ward, and soon a nurse appeared with a wheelchair. The sight of the wheelchair frightened me. For the first time I realized Nina might be in danger. I offered

116

to push the chair to the elevator. The nurse politely refused my help.

Upstairs, I waited, cursing our doctor for his tardiness. I was in a room with two expectant fathers nervously flipping the pages of magazines. The only thing I was expecting, of course, was a miscarriage. I tried to watch "The Wide World of Sports" on TV and lit four cigarettes in three minutes.

Our doctor stuck his head into the waiting room. He was a middle-aged man, and I suddenly felt guilty for disturbing his Saturday evening. He said he had seen Nina already, she would be all right, she would require a D and C, and as soon as an operating room was ready, he would perform it. Meanwhile, I could see Nina.

I went into her room; she was lying back on a pillow, her blond hair fluffed out on it. She looked like a Gainsborough girl. In her intense vulnerability she was the most beautiful I had even seen her.

"How are you feeling, baby?" I knelt down beside the bed and held her hand.

She smiled bravely, wanly, crinkling her nose. "The pain's better. They gave me something."

"And you'll soon be better, the doctor told me."

Suddenly her composure crumbled; the effort had been too much for her to sustain. Tears welled in her eyes, and she sobbed convulsively, "I've lost the baby."

"Who needed the brat?" I tried to kid.

"I'm sorry."

"It's not your fault, Nina." But I could tell that she was taking it hard. I didn't know much, but I knew something about a woman's psychology. "I read somewhere," I said, "that this is nature's way of getting rid of faulty embryos. Maybe we're fortunate in the long run."

"I'm very sleepy." Nina pressed my hand softly.

I pressed her hand back and kissed it. "Sleep, baby."

And she nodded as she dozed off.

While she was still asleep, they wheeled her out. I walked alongside her as if I were part of the hospital team that would work on her. The obstetrician looked different, more professional, in a white surgical robe. He was a person whom I had only met socially before, at cocktail parties and gatherings. Now he looked like a doctor, and I was glad of that.

"She'll be all right, doctor?" I asked.

"Of course," he said. "The only problems are psychological, possibly. But not physical. This is a very minor operation. Basically, a cleanup job." He smiled. "Nature isn't always as thorough as medicine. But Nina will be fine. And you'll be able to take her home in two or three days."

Still I was worried. I paced up and down the corridor like the relative of a Marcus Welby patient. The fact that the doctor said it was minor didn't really calm me. I knew of too many people who died undergoing minor surgical procedures. A cousin of mine died while having her face lifted. A friend in law school died having his appendix removed. An uncle of mine had gone under forever while in a dentist's chair. The thought of Nina dying overwhelmed me.

A nurse came by and told me to go to the waiting room, that I couldn't just stand around like in a Marcus Welby. I went back with the expectant fathers. They were still watching "Wide World of Sports." A demolition derby. I changed the station to the "Evening News." Then I turned it back to the demolition derby.

Our doctor came into the waiting room and sought me out.

"How is she?" I asked before he could say a word.

"Fine. Just fine. But I'll look in on her tomorrow. And I'm sure you can plan on taking her home Tuesday."

"Thank you. Thank you." I pumped his hand as if he had just completed a heart transplant. I was so relieved I clapped my hands together loudly.

"What is it?" one of the expectant fathers asked me. "A boy or a girl?"

"Neither," I called over my shoulder as I ran from the waiting room. "A wife."

But Nina was never quite the same again. It sounds corny, but something in her died when that baby never

118

got born. She was quite depressed for a while afterwards. That's when I suggested she see Dr. Hearn. She went to him for about six months. And then she broke off, saying she felt fine again. One night she confided to me, though, that she wasn't sure whether it was Dr. Hearn's help or the fact that the nine months she would have normally carried the child were over that had done the trick. "It's weird," she said, "but what was getting me down was carrying a baby that didn't exist any more. If you can understand that. I felt that my body had been geared for that purpose. And even though the baby had aborted, my body would feel it was still there. It's like my body chemistry was wound up on a special nine-month clock. And my head knew better all the time. My head could accept something and my body couldn't, if you know what I mean."

But soon Nina's head and body were together, and the incident seemed to retreat into the past. But never completely. We began to wonder about the baby that was never born and whether nature really was trying to tell us something that way. Because when we decided we'd have a child, that we wanted one, Nina couldn't get pregnant at all. We each had ourselves tested out. My sperms were healthy and plentiful. Nina's Fallopian tubes were in good order, and her eggs should have been fruitful. There was nothing wrong with either of us. But it seemed my sperm could never get through again to her egg cell.

But God, how we tried. We even went through the thermometer bit, checking Nina's cunt temperature, literally fucking by the numbers that indicated the approximate moment of ovulation, of supreme fertility. But nothing happened.

Gradually we stopped trying to have a baby. And perhaps out of frustration even the desire for a baby diminished. In addition, it was becoming a very hip thing not to have children at all. There were enough hungry babies in the world, and people pollution—or overpopulation—was a very real threat, we rationalized.

So we settled into a groove. We had no children, and that kept us young; somehow soon most of our friends were people who didn't have children, either. And our

119

lives were full with causes and friends and vacation trips. Or so it seemed to me.

But now looking out the window of my room at the Hotel Danielli, seeing a gondola bearing a couple not unlike us, I recall our second honeymoon here three years ago. Because it was then in a gondola that Nina brought up the suggestion of an adoption seriously for the first and last time. I think it was because we were so in love at the very moment, recalling all the magic of our marvelous first honeymoon here, that we wanted to sort of build a commemorative monument to our love in the person of a loved child.

Nina leaned over and kissed me. "I want to adopt a baby," she whispered. "What do you think of the idea?"

The idea didn't surprise me. It was something I knew she had been considering. She hadn't left those adoption brochures around the house for nothing. But I had always felt that the responsibility of child-raising fell most heavily on the woman, so it had to be her decision. The work, the imposition, the problems, no matter how much the man shares, are still the woman's servitude. So it wasn't for me to suggest adoption, it was up to Nina.

"Great," I said, "I love it."

"Soon as we get back, I'm going to call the agency."

The gondola rode through the slowly rippling waters. We lay back, head on arm, smiling up at the momentarily pigeonless sky.

"I feel great about it," I repeated.

A frown crossed her face, and her nose crinkled slightly. "The only thing I'm not sure about," said Nina, "is what kind of a baby."

I squeezed her affectionately and shrugged. "As long as it's healthy. That's the important thing."

Nina nodded. "But what if it's black?"

I considered the possibility. I told her honestly, "I don't think it's fair to the kid."

Nina pressed on. "What if it's brown?"

"I don't know," I began tentatively.

"Yellow?" Nina continued.

"Nina." I sat up and placed my hands on her shoulders.

120

"We can't save the world by adopting a black baby or a brown baby or a yellow baby. The world has too many big problems for us to begin to solve with the adoption of a single little baby."

"But you'll have to admit we're living a complete lie if we're afraid to do something like that," she insisted.

"Just be sure, Nina, you're not trying to be hip."

"Go fuck yourself," she said, and freed herself, pushing my hands away. Then she turned and stared sullenly at the water. I looked at the gondolier, wondering if he had spotted the sudden change in mood, the chill emotional winds now blowing across his boat. But he continued pumping away with fluid, rhythmic imperviousness.

I touched Nina's face. "I'm sorry," I said.

Nina was on the verge of tears. "You don't understand," she shook her head. "You adopt a child to make it happy."

I began to imitate romantic Italian singing, trying to cheer us both up. We laughed, as if the gestures of gaiety could artificially induce the actual emotion. But we were still a little sad in our hearts. And that sadness lingered throughout the rest of our second honeymoon. And maybe longer than that.

We never adopted a child. Now and then we brought it up, but I think we were afraid. Afraid of what? Afraid of tampering with the texture of our marriage. Afraid of unnecessarily chancing hurting each other. Afraid of spoiling what, in spite of everything, was a very good thing.

I mean, we had quarrels and disagreements, altercations and arguments—what married couple doesn't? But we didn't play brinkmanship with each other. We rarely had those cliff-hangers where you wonder if your marriage is somehow just kept hanging by a snip of Scotch Tape.

After Nina left me, I sometimes kept thinking, though, that it was the lack of a child that screwed up our marriage. But that, I decided, was a kind of sentimental cop-out. It simply was not true. What screwed up our marriage was my screwing Gloria. It was an open-and-shut case as far as Nina was concerned.

I remember, for example, the day Mrs. Cramer—the woman whose psychiatrist husband had run off with the stewardess; the woman I had glimpsed at the swingers' bar in the Valley—came back into my office. This time we were a study in contrasts. I had begun to grow my beard, and my mood was generally low. Mrs. Cramer looked like a new woman, pounds thinner, much better groomed, and she was over-brimming with happiness. She had stopped in to call off her divorce proceedings. "I'm sorry for the trouble I may have caused you," she said, as I began to show her out of my office after she told me the news.

"Don't apologize, Mrs. Cramer," I laughed. "There's nothing that makes me happier than not going through with a divorce."

"Well," she extended her hand, "thank you, Mr. Blume. And you can send the bill to my house. Jerry knows I saw a lawyer."

"There's no charge, Mrs. Cramer."

"I insist. I took your time."

"No," I shook my head. "That's our policy."

"Thank you."

I opened the door for her. "Mr. Blume . . ." she hesitated.

"Yes."

She looked me straight in the eyes, and suddenly her age showed; the weight of all her problems literally seemed to mottle the skin of her neck. Her breasts were still enormous and supple, but they seemed to heave tiredly. Still I could not avert my eyes from them.

"Do you think I'm a fool?" she was asking me.

"Why?"

"For taking Jerry back?"

"No," I quickly reassured her.

"Do a lot of women do what I'm doing?"

I put my arm avuncularly around her. "Happens all the time. Don't worry." I patted her bare shoulder. "Good luck."

"Goodbye," she said, taking in a deep breath. "And thanks again."

I watched her walk out the door, happy and exultant, and it made me sad. I called my new old secretary into my

122

office. Louise was a woman in her fifties, white-haired and skinny, who looked as if she had stepped out of a Grant Wood painting.

"Louise," I said, "you can destroy my notes on the Cramer case. And can I have a cup of coffee, please?"

"Certainly, Mr. Blume."

Louise smiled and went to fetch it for me. Women are so different, I could not help thinking; Louise and Gloria were as different as black and white. And Mrs. Cramer and Nina were just as much dead opposites. Mrs. Cramer was willing to accept her husband back, and he had done much worse than I had, running all the way off to South America for an extended fling. I had never left the Los Angeles city limits. Hell, I had never even left the house. Maybe that was my big mistake, the one thing Nina couldn't swallow. It was one thing to be unfaithful to one's wife in an impersonal motel; it was another thing to violate the sanctum sanctorum, her own personal marriage bed.

Louise brought me my coffee, placing it neatly before me on the desk, not spilling a drop. Gloria always used to splash down the coffee when she served it. So Louise was certainly a better secretary in that respect. "Thank you, Louise," I said, and watched her walk away on her thin spinster legs.

I picked up the cup of coffee and went to the window with it. In the reflection I could discern my own be-whiskered face. I rubbed my chin. If I weren't careful, I might wind up an over-age hippie, looking just like Elmo. Was I unconsciously, I wondered, growing my beard just to ape Elmo? I made a mental note: that could be something worth mentioning to Dr. Hearn. It might, as he would say, "possibly open up a fruitful avenue of discussion." I wanted Nina. Fuck fruitful avenues! I looked down at Santa Monica Boulevard with its fruitful palm trees. I saw Mrs. Cramer in a green Jaguar waiting for the light to change.

My thoughts returned to Mrs. Cramer. I envied her. Her marriage had proven more durable than mine. Perhaps it had a better foundation than mine, was built on more lasting stuff. Mine evidently had been built on quicksand.

123

Perhaps that was it. My marriage had been falling apart before Gloria ever came along. Our romp in the hay merely was the thing that shoved over an already shaky structure.

I sat down at my desk and seriously tried to address myself to that question. Was my marriage falling apart before Gloria? I strained my memory, I recalled various situations, disagreements and arguments, and finally for some reason I focused in on an incident that occurred about two years ago. Nina had become interested in yoga, and one night I accompanied her to the yoga studio for her class. She had suggested that it might do me good, too, that I certainly wasn't getting enough physical exercise shuffling divorces, that it was a better activity for my heart than the stop-and-go running in tennis.

Unfortunately the whole setup struck me as being funny. I had to manfully restrain myself from laughing. I mean everyone was so serious, trying so damned hard to be other-worldly: the fat women in leotards, the thin men in jogging outfits, everyone sitting in a circle. A lighted candle in the center of the circle. And everyone solemnly staring at the candle, meditating—or trying to meditate—while contorted uncomfortably in attempts at the lotus position. The leader, a young chick with an enormous ass, had achieved by some miracle of rubbery the perfect lotus position; my lotus, of course, looked more like a half-baked pretzel.

"Count your breath," the leader inhaled deeply. "One, two, three, four, five . . ."

I looked at Nina, and she had inhaled and was now trying her darnedest to hold her breath.

The leader continued counting, and I sneaked a fix of another breath. But Nina held her breath all the way up to the count of sixteen, when the leader said, "Exhale."

Then the exercise started all over again. And when the leader said, "Inhale," it struck me as being funny. And when I think something is funny, I laugh. Out loud.

The leader was so upset when she heard my snicker that she lost count. All the heads in the circle turned and glared at me. Including Nina's. She wouldn't forgive me for my faux pas. Evidently I had embarrassed her greatly among her yoga friends.

In the car on the way home I told her I was sorry. She just leaned against the door handle and brooded. In the house I thought I would make a peace offering. "Do you want some tea?"

"I'll make it," she said, and swept by me into the kitchen.

I couldn't sheathe my rapier-like wit. "I'll have some Yoga Herb tea," I said.

"That's not funny," Nina said, as she took the teapot down from the cabinet.

I went to the fridge and found a piece of cold chicken to nibble on. Then I went over to Nina and pecked her on the cheek. She turned her head away abruptly and ran the water. Cold water.

"Are you still angry?" I asked, not hiding the annoyance in my voice.

Nina went to the range and put the water up to boil. "I don't like when you play games," she shot back over her shoulder. "You were laughing at those people."

"Well . . ." I tried to think of an alibi. But there was no alibi. There was simply the truth, and I told her. "It was funny. Did you see the fat chick? She almost fell over. Hell, I almost fell over."

Nina measured out her words. "Why did you go, if it's funny?"

"Because I'm curious," I shrugged. "Because you suggested I go. Because you go."

She had gone to the dishwasher and was taking out cups and saucers. "Do me a favor?" She looked up. "Stay home next time."

"You're going again?" I said incredulously.

"Certainly," Nina said. "It makes me feel good." She put the cups and saucers on the table and sat down, waiting for the water to boil.

I sat down beside her. "Maybe we should get into another encounter group?" I said. And I was serious. We had gone to an encounter group a few months before, and I had felt it had done us some good. If nothing else, it had provided us with enough raw material to laugh at for a month of Sundays.

"No," Nina said, "I don't want to go to another encounter group."

"Are you afraid?" I asked. I recalled that Nina didn't exactly relish being a witness to some of the ugly spillage that sometimes resulted from lanced emotional swellings.

"No." She rose, and went to the range to get the teapot. She took a strainer, filled it with Earl Gray tea, placed it on top of the teapot and brought it to the table. "I just don't want to go to an encounter group now."

"Curt told me," I mentioned my partner, "that he and Karen are going up to Esalen for a weekend."

Nina was surprised. "Really?"

"I think," I burst out laughing, "it'll finish the marriage."

Nina poured the tea. "I don't think Karen will last more than half an hour, anyway," she allowed herself a snicker. Then she put the teapot down and slammed the table, almost toppling it. "Now I'm doing it," she said angrily.

"Doing what?"

"Putting people down."

"Karen probably *won't* last half an hour," I reminded her.

"No." Nina bit her lip and sucked in air. "We're always putting people down. You and I."

"No, we're not," I argued.

Nina did not want to argue back. "I don't know," she said, and put her head between her hands and leaned on her elbows and stared grimly ahead. "We have everything anybody could want: good jobs, a nice house, great vacations, beautiful friends—and we're both miserable."

"I'm not miserable," I insisted, and put down my chicken bone.

Nina looked up at me with watery eyes. "Are you happy?" she asked.

"I'm just not miserable," I said. "What more can anyone ask for?" I stood up and went behind her and began to knead her shoulders. "What's the matter, baby?"

"I don't know," Nina answered vacantly. But she reached up and patted my hand.

126

"Maybe you should go back to the shrink?" I ventured to suggest.

Nina pivoted her chair around. "A woman came in to see me today about her son," she said in a heavy voice. "He's a junkie. She's already on welfare. But she was trying to get more money. You want to know why?"

"I know why," I nodded. "So the son could pick up some dope."

"Yes," said Nina. "It's getting very depressing at work."

"Quit," I said.

"No. Then what would I do?"

"You could take an extra yoga class."

"That's what I mean."

"Let's go to Venice," I said.

"Let's go upstairs," she said.

I brought the dishes to the sink and deposited them there. Nina wiped the table. "Maybe *we* should give the woman some money," I said in a kidding way, even though I was searching for a way that might be helpful.

But Nina was angry. Her eyes shot sparks. "We're not committed!" she screamed accusingly and ran from the kitchen. I followed her up the stairs. The sparks had touched some fuse in me.

"What the hell do you want me to do?" I snapped hotly. "Quit my job and go to work for the Communist Party? Listen, baby, I don't need a guilt trip about money on top of everything else. I've made that journey and back the hard way."

"What does that mean?" said Nina, opening our bedroom door.

"It means," I said, "I do the best I fucking can."

Nina switched on the lights, and we both started to undress, I unbuttoned my shirt and she was stepping out of her slacks. "No, you don't do the best you can," she said, catching my eye in the mirror. "And neither do I."

I folded my pants neatly over the chair and kicked off my loafers. "I do my job," I said, standing there in my undershorts and socks. "I give to the right charities. I help the poor whenever I can. I eat. I sleep. I worry."

Nina took off her blouse and was in her leotard. She

127

picked up her hairbrush and stroked it through her hair several times. "We're both full of shit, Stephen," she said. "Just like the rest of America."

I suddenly laughed. I couldn't help it. "What's all this got to do with meditating?" I asked.

Nina put down the brush and smiled back. "I don't know," she said tiredly. "Let's go to sleep."

Nina and I had one rule. And it was a great rule. Once we got into bed, all arguments had to cease. The next morning, you could bring it up again and start anew. But bed was a moratorium for debate, a DMZ of marital warfare. We both believed fucking was too inviolate an area to fuck around with.

Nina pulled off the leotard and stood there nude. I watched her reflection in the vanity mirrors and delighted at the sight of two Ninas before me. I took off my socks and dropped my shorts and went to the real Nina and kissed her. "Do you love me?" I asked.

She wiggled her nude body against mine, pressing the contact points of skin to skin, hair to hair. Our hands fondled each other's ass. "Yes," she whispered. "I love you."

"You're a teddy bear," I mock-growled, and picked her up and carried her the few short steps to our lair, and all memories of meditation were vanquished by the overwhelming actions—or reflexes—of sex.

14

That day in my office, the day Mrs. Cramer came to tell me of her reconciliation with her stewardess-prone husband, I came to an irrevocable decision: I had to get Nina back. There was no other way, no viable alternative for me. Emotionally. Or even logically. She was the only woman I would ever love. Ever. No question about it. I would die if I didn't get her back. I did not want to die. Or, at least, go through the mechanics of dying. Therefore, I would have to get her back.

But how? That was no small problem. I mulled over it for several days and decided it was not worth mulling over. Before I could get Nina back, I would have to get *to* her. Be in her physical presence. And that I could accomplish—or at least venture—by just going to where she was. After that, I would play things by ear, improvise as I went along, depend upon the scheming side of my legally trained brain.

The next Sunday morning I went over to Nate-n-Al's delicatessen in Beverly Hills, stocked up on bagels and lox, sturgeon and whitefish, potato salad and coleslaw, and drove over to Nina's place, to my old house. I knocked on the door briskly. Nina was still in her bathrobe and was sleepily surprised to see me.

"Good morning!" I said with all the phony enthusiasm of a TV game-show host.

"What do you want?" Nina asked with justified suspicion, not moving an inch from the doorway.

"I brought bagels and lox." I extended the gift package of groceries to her.

Her arms remained folded. She was obviously pissed at me. "Come on, Blume," she said, not bothering to add: "I wasn't born yesterday. I know your tricks." But her eyes said that for her.

I replied to that message. "I came to visit Elmo," I alibied, "I like him." And I even believed what I was saying as I was saying it.

Nina was firm. She would not be moved. "I asked you in a nice way not to bother me," she warned. "And I don't want to have to ask you again."

I shifted my weight from foot to foot and did an imitation of Elmo. "It's like this," I began. "Let's get past an uncomfortable place and sort of groove where we're at. I like Elmo and he likes me and we're all in this world together. So . . ." I stopped.

Elmo had appeared in the doorway, red-eyed and looking utterly wasted, smoking his morning joint, carrying his morning cup of Yuban coffee. But there was a warm smile on his face. He seemed genuinely glad to see me.

"Far out," he smiled. "How's the man?"

And I was genuinely glad to see him. I realized at that moment how much I really liked him. I smiled back at him and answered in his own diction. "Nothin' to it."

Elmo inspected the beard on my face with approval. "You let them choppers grow and you'll look just like me."

"Yeah," I said. Then I looked at Nina earnestly, questingly, with all of the intensity of a stray, hungry dog. "Can I come in?" I asked.

Nina sighed in quiet resignation. "Yes, I guess so." Then she shook her head immediately. "Why don't I feel hostile today?" she wondered.

"Because," I said as I pushed by her, using the delicatessen for interference, "we have such a wonderful head doctor."

"No." She began to follow me toward the kitchen, yawning and scratching her head. "Because there's something wrong with my head today, I guess."

We had a great breakfast together, all of us. Bagels and lox taste ten times better with grass. And I was the autocrat presiding over the breakfast table, playing genial emcee and gracious maître d' and general all-round good fellow. Mostly, though, I was playing at being a new person, a person who had seen the light of reality and was learning to accept it. I talked about it the way a member of Alcoholics Anonymous talks about his former drinking bouts—with the enthusiasm of displaced desperation, with the fervor of a pragmatic proselytizer. I wanted to proselytize Nina into becoming a true believer in the new me.

"What's crazy is how it all changes just when you think it'll never change," I evangelized euphorically while trying to debone a whitefish and inhale from a passing joint at the same time. "I was positive it would be the way it was forever." I looked up. Elmo wasn't interested, and Nina didn't want to hear any more. "I'm not being very clear, am I?" I asked.

"How's Arlene?" Nina asked, changing the subject.

"She's fine," I said, separating most of the fish from its skeletal carriage. But then I returned to the subject, the subject of me. "I thought I would feel crazy forever," I pitched, "I thought I was having a nervous breakdown."

The joint had run down, and Elmo was bored with the direction of the conversation. He left the kitchen, a freshened cup of coffee in his hand, a beatific smile on his face. Nina looked after him, cradling her cup of coffee in two hands, as if she were being abandoned to some predator.

I continued earnestly, soberly. "I'm sorry I did what I did. Bothering you and all. Whatever . . . And I will never bother you again. You can be sure of that. But I hope we can be friends again. All of us." I indicated Elmo in the living room. "I would like that. That's all."

Nina put down her coffee and stared into it silently. "I don't know," she said finally.

I leaned across the table, and for a moment it almost seemed we were still married, late-breakfasting as usual of a Sunday morning. That sense of *déjà vu* gave me strength. "You hated me," I bluntly asked, "didn't you?"

"Yes," Nina nodded.

"And now?" I pressed on. "Do you hate me now?"

Nina smiled wanly. "I don't have time for that."

From the living room came the sound of Elmo at the keyboard of his small piano. Nina rose as if that were a signal, a cue. She went into the living room, and I followed her. I was surprised to see Nina pick up a guitar, leaning against the

131

piano, and start to tune it to the right key in order to join in with Elmo. I had never seen Nina play a musical instrument. In fact, if anyone had musical inclinations in our little married duo, it had been me.

"When did you get that?" I asked, pointing at the guitar.

Nina, concentrating intensely on the tuning process, shrugged. "After you were gone," she said; "after Elmo came."

"And you can play it already?"

She strummed it lightly and smiled up at me. "I only know chords."

Meanwhile Elmo continued beating out his funky sound, Nina backing him on her guitar, so I had to get into the act. I began to use the coffee table as a drum pad, pounding out an improvised beat with my bare hands. "This is nice," I said.

I lied, of course. It was terrible, the sound we made together, and Elmo must have known that as a professional musician. But the important thing was that I was back in business. Had I been crass? Yes. But I had also been desperate, and desperation sometimes calls for crass measures.

Anyway, we were a trio for the rest of the day. And that was the important thing.

From that day on, Nina and I were free to return to our old haunts; there was no discomfort if we ran into each other. In fact, Nina and Elmo would often let Arlene and me know where they might be going of an evening, and we'd share the intelligence of our plans with them. It was not quite double-dating, though; it was more dating duplicity on my part. I wanted to be near Nina as much as possible, and I would stoop to any subterfuge to accomplish it. If I couldn't be direct lover, I would act aimless friend. But never without a hidden purpose.

I let my hair grow longer, both from my head and from my face, and my clothing became increasingly casual. Pretty soon my evening uniform was just jeans and a pullover, and when I was with Elmo it was hard to tell who was the funky musician and who the buttoned-down lawyer by day. I can recall a particular evening during my second coming—or second acceptance by Nina—when we all arranged to meet at a party at a freaky boutique on Melrose Avenue. The clothes in the window were far out, but the people—and there were hundreds of them spilling out onto the sidewalk—were even further out of sight. They could be heard dancing inside to the sound of rock records, rapping to the smell of grass. Arlene and I, sizing up the situation, wondered if we had the shoulders to join the festivities.

Arlene looked me over disdainfully. "We fit right in," she said.

I took her arm. "Relax," I said, and began to push inside. I figured Elmo and Nina might already be there. But the doorway was so jammed we could hardly move.

A teenage girl, obviously spaced out, pressed up against me. "Can you give me a lift?" she asked.

"We just got here," I alibied.

"I gotta get out of here," she implored.

I tried to be understanding. "Oh," I said. But I could see from the weirdness in her eyes that she was too out of it to be able to really understand anything.

"The air is killing me," she continued desperately. "I've been here three days, and I broke out into a rash. See?" She turned around and lifted her blouse to reveal red pockmarks on her back.

Arlene pulled my hand. "Let's find a drink. I can use one."

The girl stuffed her blouse back into her jeans. "You should come to Hawaii," she said.

I felt sorry for the kid, so I resisted Arlene's tug. She was obviously on a bad trip, and I didn't want to make it any worse. "I've never been to Hawaii," I replied politely.

"I'm originally from here," the girl said tonelessly. "But I'm from Hawaii now. My old man is down in La Jolla opening up a juice bar, but as soon as he gets back, we're going to split for New York, then go on to Europe and North Africa, Morocco, you know, and then head back to Hawaii where you can breathe. How can you ever get your head together if you can't breathe?"

"I agree," I said. Arlene nudged me and pointed. She had spotted Elmo inside. I tried to indicate with a smile to the girl that our pleasant little conversation was over. But she gripped my arm insistently. "I think L.A. is the center of the universe," she announced.

I nodded. Why not? I certainly did not want to argue with the kid.

"It's the city of the future," she intoned solemnly, "but there's so much garbage here they'll have to push the garbage out of the center and off to the side so people can breathe."

"Right on!" I said and made my escape, squirming behind Arlene's interference. But not before I overheard the girl accosting another guy with the same come-on: "Can you give me a lift?"

Arlene and I pushed through the crowd—toward another crowd. We stepped over a dude lying on the floor, sound asleep to the world. Over him, two of his friends were discussing an unusual theological question. "Answer me, yes or no," said the shorter of the two. "Can God own land in the State of California?"

"That isn't the point," said the tall one.

The legal implications piqued me. I stopped for a second to listen.

"Certainly it's the point," the short one was saying. "It's rank discrimination against God. It's assuming He doesn't exist without proof of the fact. I have no memory of the Attorney General ever going to court to prove that God doesn't exist."

"Why does the Attorney General have to do that?"

"Because otherwise God is being deprived of His civil rights. Why shouldn't He be entitled to own land in California without at least a fair trial? Turkey is a dictatorship, for all intents and purposes, yet God is allowed to own land there."

"But that's a Moslem God," said the tall one.

"What's the difference?" The short one extended his hands palms upward. "God is God, and so the precedent has been set."

"No." The tall one shook his head. "What goes for one God doesn't necessarily apply to another God."

"But there is only one God! That's the point," the short one insisted vehemently.

I had heard enough. And fortunately Elmo had spotted

134

us. He joined us carrying two glasses of champagne, which he handed to us. "How's the man?" he asked in ritualist greeting.

I sipped the champagne and gave him the ritual reply: "Nothin' to it."

"Hey, Arlene," he hugged her warmly. "How are you?"

"Fine," Arlene smiled. She looked over his shoulder. "Where's Nina?"

"Getting it on," Elmo winked. "Getting it on." And he led Arlene out toward the dance floor in the next room. I started to look around for Nina when I felt a tap on my shoulder. I turned around. It was a teen-age boy who looked familiar. "Mr. Blume?" the boy asked.

"Yes," I said, trying to place him.

"I'm Bobby Phillips," he said. "Remember me?"

I studied his young face carefully, but I did not quite remember him. "I'm not sure I do," I admitted.

"You know my father," the boy said. "Conrad. Conrad Phillips."

I snapped my fingers. "Yeah. Yeah." I remembered now. "Connie Phillips. Sure. How is your father?"

The boy smiled sadly. "Dad sort of flipped out." He paused to partially correct himself. "Not really flipped out, exactly. He's living in a commune in Oregon. His hair is down to here." The boy indicated his own chest.

"Is he all right, though?" I asked.

The boy sighed. "He had a lot of acid. But he's okay now. At least, he's getting better."

"I hope so," I said.

"I have to send him some bread now and then," the boy reassured me, "but otherwise he's fine."

I didn't know what to say. Connie Phillips was a few years older than I. He had been in the market, working for a brokerage firm, and had had to live New York hours, getting to work before six o'clock because that's when the Stock Exchange opened there. I wondered what time he had to get up each morning at the commune. "Give him my love," I said.

"I will," the boy promised. "See you later, Mr. Blume."

I watched him push off in the direction of a mob, half wondering if the girl from Hawaii would ask him for a lift. I

135

checked the dance floor, and Elmo and Arlene were still doing their musical thing to the beat. I looked around for Nina and spotted her in a small group in a rear corner of the store, talking to an extraordinary-looking black girl in African dress. But Nina, in a long flowing tie-dyed robe, looked even more sensational herself.

She didn't notice me as I sauntered into the edge of the group. Her back was to me as she was earnestly addressing the black girl. "Are they any good, Lulu?"

"I like them," I heard Lulu reply. "They're only in super-eight. She doesn't have much money."

Evidently they were talking about films. Nina had always been something of a film freak. We both were. It's difficult growing up in L.A. and not being forever tinted with a touch of that madness.

"I'd like to see them," said Nina. "What do you think is her best one?"

"She made one that only runs about five minutes but it's my favorite. It's called *Bread*."

"Bread money?" asked Nina.

"No." Lulu laughed, showing surprisingly small teeth. "Bread bread. She baked a loaf of bread, filmed it, and then she shows what happens to the loaf of bread from start to finish. It's very funny. But it's also very heavy in its way."

"Sounds interesting," said Nina.

"It is," promised Lulu. "Wait till you see it. I'll let Jean know you're interested so the next time she has a screening she can invite you over. Or better yet, let me give you Jean's number so you can call her yourself."

"I'd love to," said Nina. "Thank you."

"Hi." I tapped Nina on the shoulder.

She turned around. The smile she had on her lips did not fade. She seemed delighted, as always lately, to see the new Blume. Little did she realize that imprisoned in the new Blume was the old Blume struggling to be unleashed. "Hi," she said, and proceeded to introduce me. "This is Lulu . . . Lulu, Stephen . . . Blume."

"Hello," Lulu nodded.

"Hello," I nodded back.

Lulu put a finger in the air and pointed at me accusingly. "Don't I know you?"

"He's my ex-husband," said Nina, with just the slightest trace of self-consciousness. But Lulu caught it.

"Oh." She laughed, and winked broadly at Nina girl to girl. "I've got a couple of exes wandering around here somewhere myself."

"This is Lulu's shop," Nina explained to me.

"It's very nice," I complimented. "What's the occasion?"

"We sold the store," said Lulu.

"Oh," I sympathized. "Business no good?"

"No," Lulu flashed her small-teethed smile again, "too good. We're just tired of working. Excuse me, have fun," she said, and started off toward another guest, who was waving to her.

Nina and I both stood there wordlessly. I pulled on my thumb like a gawky teen-ager. Nina's tongue massaged her lip. Finally she spoke first, asking, "Where's Arlene?"

"Dancing with Elmo." I pointed vaguely over my shoulder in the general direction of the dance area. "You want to dance?"

Nina immediately began to dance on the spot. I joined her. I was happy. Supremely happy. But I would not let it show on my face. Instead, I froze my face into a cool deadpan as if my gyrating body was ruled by a separate government. I could not tell what Nina was feeling—or thinking—above the neck, either. Her eyes were closed. But I knew what I was feeling—and thinking. My heart was pounding just from being so near her; the Charles Boyer vein in my forehead was throbbing. I was happier than I had been in months. I realized that I had forgotten what happiness was. At least for me. I felt alive. Passionate. Blood surged through me as if there were suddenly new Express openings in my arteries. If this was the way I'd have to spend the rest of my life, in heightened exhilaration rather than desperate anticipation, so be it, I decided.

I could have danced forever. But the record ended. And just when the next record flipped on, Lulu passed by. Nina stopped her. "Before I forget, I'd like to get Jean's number. I really want to see her."

"I have it in the back," said Lulu, and Nina followed her, leaving me standing there, watching after them wistfully. But I wasn't alone for long. I felt a light tap on my shoulder. I turned around to see who it was.

Three people stood smiling at me as if we all shared some great secret. A tall couple, both the man and the woman dressed in shredded buckskins and wearing oversized glasses, towered over a short blond girl. "Hello," said the short blond girl. "Remember me? Cindy?"

I remembered Cindy, my TV news-watching sports-fuck. "Sure, sure," I said after a moment. But I was also a little surprised and embarrassed. "What are you doing here?"

Cindy smiled. "Ed," she said, referring to the man, "sells the store their suede. Oh—" she stopped, and proceeded to introduce me all around, "Steve Babbit. This is Ed and Annie Goober." Now she leaned into me confidentially. "They're the couple I mentioned to you who are so great to swing with. Doesn't she look like a taller Twiggy?"

She didn't look like Twiggy at all. No way. "Right," I lied.

Ed nudged me in the ribs. "Far-out party."

His wife Annie put her head in close to mine. "Why don't we get out of here?"

Cindy seconded the motion. "You want to go?" she asked eagerly.

I looked around to see if anyone I knew was observing us. "I really can't," I said as if I were heartbroken at the fact. "I'm here with a date."

"Five is okay," shot back Cindy, with Annie and Ed nodding in agreement.

"I'm awful sorry," I said. "Maybe some other time. Excuse me." I held up my hand as if someone were calling me from across the room and beat a hasty retreat.

No one had been calling me, of course. Except I could not bear being away from Nina for too long whenever I had the opportunity to be in her presence. I knew I had to make every second count. I hated to waste one golden moment. She was the sun, and my life revolved around her. I fitted my orbit into her plans, I adjusted my life to her schedule much more than I had ever done when we were married. Not being able to see her at will, I had to see her by means of will.

Because if I did not see her a single day I would ache to the point of pain, I would become depressed to the point of numbness, and I would spend a night alternating between non-feeling and overpowering feeling. When I was with her, I operated at a feverish pitch, my body mass-producing adrenalin so I could brightly sparkle at all times. But if I was away from her for an extended period I quietly became hysterical. It was hell on my chemistry.

Fortunately, though, I was seeing more and more of Nina and Elmo. Elmo always remained the same. He had the quality of a shaggy old dog in that he never seemed to change at all. What I mean is this: see Elmo one night, go off to work and a hard day at the office, and see Elmo the next night, and it was as if no time had passed in the interval. Elmo could even pick up a conversation where it had left off the night before without missing a beat. For Elmo had successfully banished—or vanquished—time. Just as it was an element that he simply refused to acknowledge, he seemed to be able to pass through it impervious to its usual assaults. Which gave him, in spite of his unstable behavior according to the usual social standards, a great aura of security. You knew in his offbeat way that you could always be sure of Elmo.

Nina had changed. She was happier, freer, more her own person. Whether it was because of Elmo's presence, or because of my absence, or because of Dr. Hearn's magical listening elixir, she seemed to have shed both physical years and intellectual pretense as a result of shedding me. She looked younger and acted younger, she was less concerned with what other people were thinking and more concerned with her own feelings. She had always been honest; now she was direct, too. Aside from the fact that I still loved her, I also liked her more than I ever had before. Which didn't make things any easier for me either.

But she accepted my presence without making me feel like an intruder. Night after night we'd sit around the living room in Laurel Canyon, the fireplace lit, Elmo rolling the grass, Nina strumming the guitar, old new Stephen breaking open a few bottles of wine, and just quietly rap, while cozily getting stoned. We'd talk about lifestyles and places to live and values to have. It was like the kind of sessions I used to have in college dorms, but now the participants brought with them some worldly experience. We'd all been to a few places and tried a few things.

At first, Arlene would come along with me to Laurel Canyon. But gradually it was plain that she didn't belong, that it wasn't her scene. So the foursome became an at-home threesome. But I still kept seeing Arlene—in bed. At the dog end of the evening I would wend my way up to her place, or she'd bring her tail down to mine.

That makes it seem like I was having the best of two possible worlds, but in reality it sometimes tore the innards out of me. I mean, having been with Nina all evening, I did not exactly embrace Arlene with the greatest enthusiasm. The better the evening would be with Nina and Elmo, the worse the gray morning would become with Arlene. It was as if the spirit could devour the flesh.

I remember one night—a few nights before I came to the end of my rope—Elmo and Nina and I were sitting around. We were talking about Europe and the expatriate life. Elmo had never been to Europe, and he sat on the floor, sucking in on his joint, like a curious student, a disciple anxious to learn. Nina was putting down the Paris scene. "All I know," she said, reaching for the joint and inhaling deeply, "is everyone who goes there comes back. Sooner or later they come back. At first they're enthralled with the life, but then after a few years it gets to them. I think it's the same living in any other country. Eventually, you want to come back. No matter what's wrong here, you can't hack it there. Look at Timothy Leary. He wanted to get busted, I'm sure. He didn't want to settle down in Afghanistan. He preferred facing jail again here. And the same with Eldridge Cleaver. From all I hear, he wants to come back here."

"They're different," I argued. "You're talking about people who because of their politics—and the advocacy of grass is a political position—had no choice but to get out of this country. Eldridge and Leary didn't choose to live abroad. They were forced to go abroad. So they couldn't just live casually wherever they lived.

140

"But what I mean is, after a trip to Europe, when I come back here, I always miss the way of life over there. It's just nice to have a café to sit at. To see people. To be aware of the flow of people. You just don't see people in this country. You see automobiles. So imagine how good it can be—having that human experience—for several years."

I took my drag on the joint and passed it back to Elmo.

Nina sipped thoughtfully on her wine and shook her head. "The point I'm trying to make, Stephen, is that if your head is good here, it's good there. If your head is not good, it's no good anywhere. Maybe Cleaver and Leary were bad examples. But I was trying to use them to show that it simply isn't only this country that's the problem. That's a cop-out."

"I still don't agree with you," I replied. "I don't think it's a cop-out to go live in another country. We're all social animals, we live in a community—or what's supposed to be a community—and we're affected by it. If everybody you know spends their life watching television and bullshitting about how bad the air is, you find yourself doing the same thing."

Nina shrugged and picked up her guitar. Elmo took a last drag on the joint before tamping it out. "I'd like to go to Morocco," he smiled, looking at me.

"I've never been there," I said.

"Tell you the truth," said Elmo, "the best place I ever lived in was Bayonne, New Jersey."

I laughed.

"I mean it," Elmo grinned back. "When I was a kid. Not later. But I mean when I was a kid we had the whole scene worked out. Front porch. Backyard. And we had a goat."

Nina began to strum on the guitar, providing Elmo with a pastoral musical underscore. "The goat," Elmo reminisced, "fuckin' goat was beautiful. His name was Chester. Chester the goat." Elmo picked his nose and laughed. "My Uncle Chester gave him to us. Uncle Chester was a farmer. Tomato farmer. And anyway, about six o'clock every day, we'd all sit around on the front porch and get it on. Not much talking. Just a lot of sitting and rocking and waving and smiling and milk and cake . . . Man, it was something."

Nina began to sing softly, improvising as she went along:

"Sitting around doing nothing . . .
    Sitting around going nowhere . . .
    Sitting around with our family . . ."

Elmo went to his little piano and gave the tune some body
and Nina sang it again:
"Sitting around doing nothing . . .
    Sitting around going nowhere . . .
    Sitting around with our family . . ."
and I joined in, supplying a fourth line:
"Strumming the old banjo . . ."
We all laughed, and Elmo picked up his trombone and
Nina started another verse:
"Sitting around on the front porch . . .
    Sitting around in the backyard . . ."
"Sitting around in New Jersey," I sang out,
    Sitting around in Bayonne . . ."
and the three of us were into it together, singing that song,
making up preposterous verses, but feeling as close as three
people can feel. If I ever loved a man, it was Elmo that
night. And I know Nina loved me that night, too. It was as
if the three of us were enclosed in a circle of love. And none
of us could avoid it.

When I went home, I held out my hand and it was trem-
bling. It trembled from the restraint I had put on it. Being so
near Nina, feeling so much toward her, sensing her own vibes
toward me, and yet not being able to touch her, forcing back
every natural and normal and healthy impulse I had was
taxing the electricity in my nervous system to the limit. I
couldn't go on like this. It was torturous going on like this.
But not seeing Nina, not getting *that* close to her, was a
hundred times worse. Either alternative was untenable. I
knew I was reaching the breaking point.

But I didn't talk about it to Dr. Hearn the following day.
Instead, I talked around it. "I know she knows I love her—
there's no way I can really hide it. I know she feels something
for me—there's no mistaking it. The only thing I don't know
is exactly what it is she's feeling. Maybe it's just repressed
anger and I'm mistaking it for another emotion. But she is

142

feeling something. How the hell can she accept me and not feel anything? . . . Does that make sense?"

"What do you think?" asked Dr. Hearn, tapping the pencil against his mouth.

"I think it makes sense," I said, "but maybe you can help me in this area. That is if you're willing to answer something. But perhaps I shouldn't ask you this. I know. There's no *should*," I quickly corrected myself. "But this is a question of ethics. For you." I drew in a deep breath and used my best trial cross-examination voice. "Before she stopped seeing you, what did Nina say about me?"

The pencil stopped. Dr. Hearn was shaking his head reprovingly. "You know I won't answer that," he said in a tone of great personal disappointment, "so why did you ask?"

I was deflated. I tapped my heel on the floor. I put my hands over my eyes. "Maybe I should quit, too? Stop seeing you completely."

"Mmm," Dr. Hearn nodded.

"Does *that* make sense?" I ventured.

"Well, let's talk about it. What are your feelings about that?"

"I don't know," I leveled, "I want to. I'm not sure, though."

"Why don't we finish the month out," Dr. Hearn rubbed his nose with the pencil, "and see how it goes?"

But I was too frustrated and too hostile to let him off that easily. He hadn't given me what I wanted, so I was intent on giving him a hard time.

I stood up. "I'm beginning to think all of this is a waste of time." I indicated the office, the diploma on the wall, the doctor himself. "That it's all a crock. That it doesn't really work."

"Sometimes," Dr. Hearn smiled airily, "I'm inclined to agree with you."

I was surprised at his quick agreement. "Then why do you do this?" I wanted to know.

"Until we find something better," Dr. Hearn rose wearily, "what else is there to do?"

We looked at each other for a long time. And then he

showed me out of the office and reminded me of the time and day of our next appointment.

And at our next appointment I had a lot to talk about. Because the next night I did something I never dreamed I would ever do in all my wildest fantasies. And I did it to Nina.

15

I didn't plan it, exactly. It just worked out that way. But perhaps it was inevitable, the last act in the comedy drama of myself that I was acting out as the new Stephen, the friendly Stephen, the all-understanding Stephen. I drove up Laurel Canyon in my 2002 not realizing that my head was actually more far out than anything in *2001,* because I was on an odyssey of inner space, the really uncharted terrain of the future. As Dr. Hearn said, we know so little of how the mind works. Especially one's own mind. If you asked me that evening where I was going and what I was planning to do, I would have gestured aimlessly and said, "I'm going to drop in on my friends Elmo and Nina and smoke a little grass and blow a little music and just sort of be friendly together." Which, in effect, was what I told Arlene I was going to do. And driving up the canyon I was, in fact, playing around with that verse of musical doggerel that we had put together two nights before:

"Sitting around on the front porch,
  Sitting around in the backyard,
  Sitting around in the toilet . . .
  Strumming my old banjo . . ."

I felt also as if I had everything under control. I was doing pretty much what I wanted to do, getting a chance to spend another evening with Nina. I knew there were pitfalls, I knew there was an excruciating price that I would have to pay for that small but immensely pleasurable experience, but I assumed I could handle it. After all, I had handled it up to then, hadn't I? Why should I have expected it to be any different that night?

I was so sure of the cordial—or better than that, matter-of-fact—welcome I would receive, I did not even bother to call and say I was coming. And as I parked my car in the familiar driveway I was even planning to spring a new verse on Elmo and Nina.

"Sitting around the pool . . .
 Sitting around the patio . . .
 Sitting around in California . . .
 Sitting around in Brentwood . . ."

I gave a Fred Astaire kind of knock, jaunty-like, on the oak door. Nina opened the door. She was wearing a fiery red blouse and jeans. "Elmo isn't here," she announced.

"I should have called," I apologized. "Where is old Elmo?"

"He went to a movie."

"Oh," I said, and perhaps I should have turned around and left then and there. Perhaps it would have been better in the long run for all of us. But I didn't. I had worked too hard to even consider staging a momentary strategic retreat of any sort. I had established my beachhead, and I was not about to abandon it so lightly. I shrugged, as if to say as long as I'm here and I don't know what else to do, I might as well stay here, anyway. "Can I come in?" I asked.

In reply Nina stepped back to let me pass and shut the door behind me. But she also let me know that she was letting me stay *there* more than stay with *her*. "I'm practicing on my guitar," she said, as she led the way into the living room. And then she picked it up, curled up on the sofa, and began to strum some notes on it. I sat down in the peacock chair across the room and listened attentively. Damn it if she wasn't getting better. Her understanding of the instrument was passing from a forced mechanical one to an unconscious feeling one. She and the guitar were on the verge of having a reciprocal relationship, the necessary takeoff point for creative music-making.

"You're really improving," I complimented her.

"I practice a lot," she murmured, without looking up, intent on her fingering.

"I'll fix myself a drink," I said.

"There's a joint if you want it." Nina pointed to the ashtray on the coffee table before her.

146

I went over, picked it up, lit it, and took a first lung-filling, soul-bracing drag. Now I wanted the drink even more. I started toward the kitchen. "I still think I'll have a drink," I said. "Anything for you?"

Nina shook her head and continued to strum, as if the guitar were the only pick-me-up she would ever need. But I was getting used to drinking a lot, maybe because Arlene was a borderline juicer. Arlene could hold her liquor, but she certainly drank quantities of it. And the least I could do sometimes was serve as her drinking partner.

In the kitchen I took a started bottle of Scotch from the liquor cabinet. It was my brand. I noticed that most of the apéritifs and brandies were stuff still left over from when I had lived there, from my stock. Perhaps that was another reason I felt so comfortable moving about the kitchen, opening the fridge, taking out the ice tray and dumping its contents into the ice bucket I found in the familiar place, the cabinet beneath the silver drawer. Yes, I certainly knew my way around the kitchen, at least that kitchen. I poured myself a healthy shot, put in two ice cubes, and swished it around. Then I took another heady puff on the joint before taking my first sip of the Scotch. It was great. Scotch and grass; what a wonderful taste sensation. Somebody could get rich packaging it. And call it Scotch and Heather.

Still smiling at my little joke, I returned to the living room. I sat back and made myself comfortable. Nina was still playing and singing. The song she was singing was "You've Got a Friend . . ." There was an untutored quality, a natural and unpretentious tone in her voice that I loved. I was comfortable. I could listen to her sing all day. I took another drag on the joint and offered her a puff on it before I snuffed it down. She shook her head and continued singing. Which was fine with me.

"You're really good," I said in genuine admiration. And I smiled my enjoyment of her music to her.

She finished the song and held out the guitar and yawned. "So," I held up my glass as if to toast her, "what's new?"

Nina stifled another yawn. "What do you mean?"

"How's your job?" I asked.

"The state is cutting down on our funding. All the way

147

across the board," she sighed. "Some of our best programs may soon be zilch."

"That's too bad," I sympathized. I knew how much Nina cared about her work.

"That's our Governor," she said resignedly.

I was frankly more concerned about her fate than that of the entire welfare program. "But there's no danger of you losing your job, is there?" I asked.

"No." She clicked her tongue against her teeth as if to indicate it would be better if she did lose her job and the money were given to someone in dire straits. "No," she repeated, "I just won't have any money to give to people."

That seemed to end our conversation. I didn't want it to end. I tried to pump new life into it—or rather, to extend its life. "Has the devaluation affected things?" I asked.

Nina laughed bitterly. "The poor are always devalued. Hasn't changed. And maybe it'll never change. It's still the same old mess. Only worse."

Her tone was getting depressing. I didn't want to depress her or myself. I switched the topic. "What flick did Elmo go see?"

Nina smiled. *"Gone with the Wind."*

I laughed. "He's never seen it before?"

It was Nina's turn to laugh. "He's seen it about ten times," she said.

"Then why go see it again?"

"Elmo says he knows it's good. That's why he goes to see it over and over again. He knows the script, I think, word for word. I went with him once and watched his lips move in exact sync to Clark Gable's voice."

"I think I like Elmo," I said in genuine appreciation, "as much as any man I've ever known."

Nina nodded. "He's a . . ." she paused to search for a word and settled on, "card."

I leaned forward and asked her straight out. "Do you love Elmo?"

Nina considered my question seriously. "Sometimes," she decided. "Yes. Sometimes I love him a lot."

"When don't you love him?"

Nina rubbed her chin thoughtfully. "When he runs out

of dope, he can be very crazy," she said finally. "And when he's selfish . . ."

This surprised me. "I didn't think Elmo could be selfish."

Nina looked at me as if I were a foolish schoolboy. "I don't know anyone who isn't selfish sometimes."

I was ready to argue. But only for the sake of a joke. "Norman Mailer," I suggested.

Nina laughed. Oh, how I loved to see her laugh. Some people just laugh with their lips, their faces. Nina laughs with her whole body, her shoulders shaking, her breasts bouncing, her whole being participating in an act of enjoyment. "The Pope," I continued to list unselfish people, "Richard Milhous Nixon."

"He's not selfish," Nina said wryly, "he's just misunderstood."

"Like me," I allowed.

"You're not misunderstood," Nina lowered her voice for dramatic effect. "You're perfectly clear."

I emptied my drink, sucking in on an ice cube. "Am I?" I put the glass down on the end table.

Nina narrowed her eyes and shook her head. "I see right through you, Blume."

There she was, going with that Blume again. Suddenly we were resuming an adversary relationship. One slip, one self-indulgence, and I was in danger of blowing my whole cover. "What do you see, kid?" I asked, rolling my lips, doing a Humphrey Bogart imitation.

Nina ignored my attempts at high jinks this time. "I see a man," she leveled, but in a smug, self-satisfied tone, "who is trying to worm his way back into my good graces and who, parenthetically, will not ever really succeed."

I switched over to W. C. Fields. "Then why do you permit me to be here, my little chickadee?"

Nina curled back. "If I knew why I did all the things I do, I would have saved about thirty thousand dollars at the shrink."

"You mean," I corrected her, "*I* would have saved about thirty thousand dollars."

Nina gestured with her hand as if to say the thirty thousand dollars was immaterial, beside the point. Her voice became gentler. "I want to be free and open and clear about all my relationships," she began. "I don't want to feel hatred for anyone if I can help it. I want to be my own person. All the time. Do you understand?"

I nodded. "I think so."

"All right," she continued. "Now you're part of my past. No," she stopped and corrected herself, "you're part of my present, too. What I mean is: so we were married and we got divorced and you're here now and I don't hate you any more and I don't love you any more. And I feel good about myself."

She struck a chord on the guitar to punctuate the end of her speech. I accepted her speech, but I wasn't too sure of it at the same time. For someone who was trying to be her own person, Nina sounded too much like Dr. Hearn talking in the diction of Elmo. But I had heard her out. And now I thought it was my turn. "Do you want to hear how I feel?" I asked.

Nina looked away. "Not particularly," she said.

I stood up. "I'm fixing another drink. You want one?"

"What are you drinking?"

"Scotch." I held up the empty glass as if that somehow indicated its drained contents.

"I'll have Scotch and water."

I walked toward the kitchen, but I stopped for a moment before the sofa. "When I come back, I'll tell you how I feel, anyway," I promised—or threatened.

Nina picked up her guitar and began to play "Hey, Jude." I poured our drinks in the kitchen, sensing a mounting tension. Nina may have been calmly stroking her guitar while I was casually clinking ice cubes into glasses, but these were just the bravado warmup exercises of adversaries before a confrontation. Nina and I were heading toward a showdown as surely as Gary Cooper ever stalked a gunfighter down a Western street. Only we were sophisticates, urban sophisticates, and our badges were our watered-down drinks, our intelligent airs, our indifferent facades. But we were in deadly earnest. At least, I was. I was fighting for my life.

I returned with the drinks, and Nina indicated that I was to put her Scotch on the coffee table. She was still too involved in playing the bridge of "Hey, Jude." I sat down and sipped my drink. "I want you to know how I feel," I announced.

Nina looked away, strumming her old guitar, as if what I had to say was not of the least bit of concern to her. That old deadly shield of indifference. It was meant to be off-putting, but it didn't put me off. I had waited too long to say what I was going to say. Somewhere in my unconscious, I believe, I had even rehearsed it—if such a process is possible.

"Of course," I began, biting my lip, "I'm still in love with you. But that you know. So there's no point in going over that. Just let me say that I love you now in a way that is completely different from the way I loved you before. Maybe it's because you're not mine any more. Not that you were ever really *mine*. You didn't belong to me." I stopped. "No, that isn't exactly the truth, and I have to be absolutely truthful."

I continued in an even voice. "I guess in a way you did belong to me, and that's what was wrong. Yes, it was wrong. You shouldn't have belonged to me. Of course, it wasn't just my fault. You must have wanted to belong to someone, or else you would've done something about it."

I sipped my drink. As if on cue, Nina picked hers up and sipped it, too. "All the chicks," I continued, trying to establish eye contact with her, but failing, "all the chicks who claim we made them slaves have been digging the slave trip. Now they're waking up, and it's a good thing. I'm in favor of woman's liberation. I'm in favor of man's liberation. I'm in favor of anyone's liberation so that he—or she—can best fulfill himself on his—or her—own terms. And no one has the right—mother or father, husband or wife, son or daughter—to run anyone else's life as if it were an adjunct of his—or her—own life, like a trailer connected to a rear bumper, something secondary or behind."

Now I emptied my glass in one swig. And said what my heart cried out. "So anyway, my little chickadee . . ." I tried to self-mock but it was no good and I stopped and used my own natural voice, almost being able to hear the tremors in it as I spoke. "I love you. Completely. Totally. Every second. Every day.

"When I fuck Arlene," I even confessed, "I see you. Oh, yeah," I nodded. "Always."

Nina began to play that Dylan song "Blowing in the Wind."

"You come in loud and clear," I nodded. But I couldn't stop there. I had to tell her everything, I couldn't hold back anything. "Arlene knows about it," I continued, "and she has come to accept it as part of life. You see, Arlene is still essentially a slave. She says she can't help it. She feels sorry for herself. And I feel sorry for her. But that's the way it is." I shrugged helplessly.

Nina seemed more intent on her music than on listening to me. I had to shake her out of her cool. "Do you ever see me when . . ." I hesitated, "when you're with Elmo?"

Nina stopped singing just long enough to utter one sharp word. "Never." And then went right back to her singing.

"Funny," I noted as much to myself as to Nina, "I couldn't bring myself to say 'fuck' about you and Elmo . . ." And I tried to joke it off. "You don't really do it, do you?" I held up my hand. "Don't answer."

She didn't answer.

My glass was empty. But I had still saved some of the joint. I relit it, took a leisurely drag, and then dropped my penultimate weapon, a verbal blockbuster. "So the real question is," I said quietly, but leaning forward intently, "am I going to bed with you tonight?"

The bomb exploded the room into silence. Nina stopped playing and put down the guitar. "Go home, Blume," she said in measured tones.

I laughed. "This is my home."

"Please," she urged.

I shook my head. "You have nothing to be afraid of, Nina. You're not a slave," I said, and went into my FDR voice: "The only thing you have to fear is fear itself."

I went to join her on the sofa. She uncurled, sprang to her feet, and ran to the chair where I had been sitting. I returned there and bowed down at her feet.

"I want to kiss you," I pleaded sincerely.

"No," she said, a hint of fear now in her voice. She knew I was for real. In every way.

152

That gave me courage in a perverse way. "What's the difference?" I continued. "If you don't love me. What's the difference? Just one kiss."

"The difference is, Blume," said Nina hotly, "I don't want to."

"Yes, you do," I insisted. "Or you wouldn't have let me in here in the first place."

"I always knew you were a tricky bastard, Blume," she spit back.

There was a choke in my throat, and I swallowed it down. Tears crept into the corner of my eyes and I blinked them away. "I love you so much my heart is breaking," I whispered hoarsely.

"Please," said Nina very quietly. "Go home."

"Please," I whispered just as quietly. "Just one kiss?"

From out of nowhere came Nina's right, clenched in a fist, landing low and hard, right in my gut, knocking me over flat on my back. I was more surprised than hurt as she rushed past me toward the stairs. I quickly got to my feet and chased after her, warning, "Now I want it all!"

If you had asked me that afternoon whether there was the slightest possibility that I would ever rape Nina, I would have dismissed the question as absurd and ridiculous, saying that there wasn't even the remotest chance that I would ever rape anyone—let alone Nina. Violence has never been my bag. Brutality to me is about as sexually stimulating as a cold shower. I have never found sadism or masochism erotic in any shape, manner, or form. Beat me and I cry. Ask me to beat someone else, and I will cry, too—for that person. I like neither to inflict nor to suffer pain. Pleasure is my thing, and I take it straight.

But when Nina ran up the stairs, I chased after her. I chased her for reasons of tenderness—believe it or not—with the emotion of love uppermost in my heart. But she raced into the bedroom as if I were some monster and tried to shut the door in my face. I did not want her to reject me, I wanted to show her how much I adored her. I got one foot wedged in the door and with that as purchase, pushed my way into the room. Nina retreated behind the bed as if it could serve as a protective barricade. I inched slowly around the edge of the bed toward her.

"Don't be crazy, Blume," she implored as she backed into the night table.

"Ah, there's the rub," I threatened, "I am crazy." And, of course, I was crazy. But crazy only with love.

Nina picked up the lamp from the night table and brandished it before her. Obviously, she was scared. "Get the fuck out of my house," she warned.

I lunged at her. She threw the lamp. I ducked, and it smashed noisily to the floor. I grabbed her. She tried to push me away, scratching and flailing, but I was too strong, pinning her down on the bed, our bed, and holding her there. Her expression was one of utter vulnerability, her blond hair lying back loosely as it framed her blanched, frightened face, reminding me of the way she had looked in the hospital when she had the miscarriage.

"I love you," I said.

Her fists, exerting power only from her restrained wrists down, beat up against my chin. But her smell, the lovely Nina smell, wafting toward me, was actually more capable of overpowering me.

"Love you . . . Love you . . . Love you," I repeated, trying to kiss her constantly wiggling head. Finally I pressed my lips atop hers. And she bit down viciously. That hurt me. And I could taste the blood. But not as keenly as I had tasted Nina.

I snuggled in to kiss her neck. She resisted me. I ripped her blouse. She managed to free one hand and punched me in the back repeatedly like a fighter caught in a clinch. I kissed her breasts, her lovely glorious breasts that were like nourishment to me, tearing away the obstructing bra with my teeth. It was then that I heard Nina crying.

I tried to soothe her. "You're so sweet. You're so lovely," I whispered. "And, oh, your fucking skin is like velvet."

She stopped defending herself, and I felt that she was feeling as I was feeling, that her body was getting the message from mine. I relaxed the pressure I had been exerting on her legs, leaning back on my ankles, freeing her momentarily.

Nina took advantage. She kicked me viciously in the balls and I reached over and clutched myself there in pain. Nina bounced off the bed and ran from the room.

I leaped after her, chasing her down the hallway and the stairs again, and I caught her at the foot of the stairs, tackling her hard, bringing her down on the floor, her naked tits completely exposed to me now. I rubbed my head into them and began to wiggle out of my pants at the same time.

"You're sick, Blume," Nina sobbed.

"Has to be, baby," I reassured her. "Has to be." And I meant it. I was crazy, yet I was calm at the same time. I knew that no outside force or demon had seized control of me. I merely felt that what I was about to do was the most natural thing in the world for me to do. If that's being psychotic, then I was psychotic, but I did not feel psychotic at all. I knew exactly what I was doing. And I knew nothing in the world could stop me from doing it. If ever I had been caught up in a chain of inevitability, it was at that moment.

Still Nina tried to get up, to push me off. I pushed her back again. She stopped sobbing. She became calmer. It was as if she, too, were suddenly resigned to the inevitable. The fight had oozed out of her. Kissing her nipples, I unzipped Nina's jeans and slipped them down, my hand massaging the mound above her cunt.

"Let me get my diaphragm," she whispered.

My pants were off now, her jeans were down, and it was too late for that. "Do you know how much I love you?" I asked as I mounted her there on the floor.

Nina did not answer. But neither did she fight back. I still held her hand, ready to twist it painfully.

"You're my teddy bear," I said, pressing my prick against her cunt.

Nina sucked in air. "I'm a statue, Blume," she warned.

But little by little, gradually, inevitably I was inching my way in. "Such a soft statue," I whispered, Nina's legs spreading wider and my prick sliding in deeper. And soon Nina's cunty juices were sweetly lubricating my way. And it was as if our bodies had been waiting for the moment, primed for the moment, remembering in the nucleus of each cell the great intimacies we had shared. If Nina's conscious mind hated me, the unconscious governors of her body welcomed me, treating me as some long-desired and revered friend. And as with an old friend, no preliminaries were really necessary. Our bodies were ready to pick up just where they had left off. Our bodies nursed no grievances, remembered no hurts. But much more surprising was the fact that they seemed capable in concert of producing what I can only describe as instant foreplay. I was as aroused and as excited as if we had been erotically cultivating each other for hours. And so, too, was Nina. Her arms, her hands, her legs, reluctantly, then enthusiastically, embracing me and enveloping

156

me, accepting me. She was not for an instant affectionate, but she was not dispassionate, either. And I was amazed, consciously amazed, to realize that though I had forced my way in, I might bring her off. For her breathing was becoming heavier, quicker, her sounds increasingly were the inescapable moans of pleasure. I slowed down the pace of my thrusts mechanically, counting numbers precisely to myself, even for one split second considering the possibility of thinking of Arlene. I wanted to be sure Nina had an orgasm. If I was a rape artist, then I was going to be an artist as much as a raper. I was going to be the most considerate raper in history; I was going to make sure my Nina came.

But as Nina's excitement grew so, too, did mine; making love is a contagious process, and soon I was holding on, exquisitely denying myself one more moment of pleasure for the promise of the next moment, when Nina began to churn away beneath me, forcing the issue, the horse commandeering the jockey, for the final ride home, and gasping screaming, biting, calling out my name, yes, not Blume, not even Steve, but "Stephen," "Stephen," "Stephen," "yes," as only she could say it, yes, and then I was letting go, letting go completely, feeling grand release, great surcease, waves of peace, as I had not experienced in all the lovemaking I had done since I last made love to Nina. For this was love. Real love. Not sex or fantasy. But something as real as the desire to live, as the desire to create life, as the desire to nourish the goodness in oneself forever.

When we heard the sound of the door opening, Nina and I, still catching our breaths, looked at each other, an intense two inches away, the short-angle lenses of the eyes taking in every flickering detail; and then simultaneously, our heads turned to the door, the direction of the sound, and by that time our long-angle lenses were in focus, grinding away.

Elmo seemed tall, gigantic, framed in the doorway, silently looking down at us. He was surprised, but not stunned. No trace of great disgust or puritan shock or personal betrayal showed on his face. There was a hint of anger—but only for a moment. Or perhaps he was too hurt to really show his anger.

"You all sure missed a good movie," he finally said in a mock Southern accent.

Nina turned away. I jumped to my feet and pulled my pants on. Elmo didn't seem interested in me at all. His eyes never left Nina. She was retrieving her clothes and covering, rather than dressing, herself with them.

"Time for me to split?" Elmo asked her calmly.

Nina faced him, shaking her head, pointing up at me accusingly. "He raped me."

"Did you dig it?" Elmo wanted to know. He had yet to take his eyes off Nina.

Nina started to cry. "He really raped me," she repeated.

Elmo nodded. He closed the door behind him and walked over to me. "Is that the truth?"

"Yes."

Elmo shook his head, like a schoolmaster disappointed in a student he had overrated. "It's bad, chief," he decided. "Fucking has to be mutual from the start."

Then he punched me in the face, a hard hook that landed on my cheek. And while I was beginning to feel the pain, he unloaded a right to my stomach, doubling me over. But I did not try to defend myself. I let him punch away, feeling the blows rain down on my head, knowing I deserved them, my senses becoming more alert, rather than dulled through pain.

If pain began to show anywhere it was on Elmo's face. Each time he hit me, he seemed to become angrier and angrier. And soon the anger screwed its way into the contorted mask of pain.

When Elmo realized how angry he had allowed himself to become, how much hurt he had let his chemically protected soul feel, he stopped pummeling me and began to cry. Nina was sobbing on the floor near our feet. And I was bawling, too. Not for myself. Not even for Nina. But for what I had driven Elmo to do.

I put my arms around Elmo to comfort him. But Elmo could no longer control himself. Intense emotion had seeped into his overly sensitive soul. He broke down completely.

Nina stood up and tried to comfort Elmo, too. So there we were, the three of us standing there, Nina and I each hugging Elmo from the side, Elmo wailing like a wounded gentle animal, each crying in his own way, but the three of us joined together helplessly, emotionally welded by the force of love.

As we gradually calmed down, I thought for sure that Nina would call the police. Seek some sort of immediate retribution. But she became very calm. Ultra calm.

She pushed me away from Elmo and herself. Closed me out of the temporary corporation. "You're a sick animal, Blume," she said. "You need help. Go see a doctor."

I moved toward the door. Elmo was still in her arms. She poked her head around his shoulders. "And, Blume . . ." she called out.

I stopped, my hand on the doorknob.

"Don't ever come back," she threatened, her head moving slowly from side to side.

I opened the door and left the house. In the driveway I noticed the garbage can knocked over, its contents strewn about. Evidently a raccoon had got to it. I replaced everything in the container, except for a tomato juice can. I kicked it as hard as I could and watched it roll down the Canyon road, its lonely sound producing a thunderous reverberation in the otherwise quiet night.

17

Having had what I wanted on one level, I was now living on the sharp edge of a razor. No matter which way I held it, it cut. And hurt. My world had fallen apart. But, if it was any solace, so too had everybody else's. Or at least everybody else I encountered during the next few weeks. It was as if a cosmic signal had gone out to all the sinking ships at sea: list to Blume. He's listing himself, so he'll listen.

The first client to come into my office the next day, for example, was Ed Goober, the husband of Twiggy Annie Goober, the swinging sensation of two valleys. Ed was wearing another of those shredded wheat buckskin Western outfits I had seen him in at the party at Lulu's. But if that night he seemed a cool dude of sexual mystery, in my office he was an angry man in marital misery. He ranted and raved incoherently, and I tried to calm him down. Rubbing the bruises Elmo had inflicted on my swelled face, I reminded him sorrowfully, "Anger won't get you anywhere."

"Sorry," he apologized abjectly, "I didn't mean to take it out on you, I just feel so lousy about it. I'm angry at her. Not you."

"I understand, Mr. Goober," I replied professionally.

"Call me Ed," he said just as professionally, the salesman in him coming to the fore. "I mean, don't you think I'm right?"

"I'm here just to handle your divorce, Ed," I explained, "I'm not here to get into who's right and who's wrong."

Ed Goober saw my point and smiled. "I don't blame you." But he still wanted me to see his point. "But if you live seven years with a chick," he argued, "and you both swing and you both get it on and she suddenly decides she doesn't

160

want to swing, you got a right to get upset, wouldn't you say?"

"What you're saying," I tried to translate his complaint into legal terms, "is that you're incompatible."

"Incompatible?" His eyebrows shot up into the brim of his ten-gallon hat. "You bet your life we're fucking incompatible. Out of the clear blue sky she tells me she wants a one-on-one relationship." He shook his head disbelievingly. "I think she's flipped. I worked seven years with this chick to loosen up her skull, and now she wants a square sex scene."

I tried to sympathize—or at least help him find solace. "Do you have any children?" I asked.

"Yeah," he nodded, "we got six kids."

I laid out the groundwork for the Goober divorce. I began to see it all as a comedy. Maybe I was just consoling myself with someone else's pain. But it helped me get through the morning.

Coming back from lunch, I ran into my partner Curt on the elevator. I had been avoiding his inquisitive glances all morning. But now we were forced to make conversation on the ride up. I said nothing after the preliminary greeting and the usual observation about the smog. But Curt, after pushing the button for our floor, stepped back and came right to the point.

"I've been polite all morning, Stephen," he said. "Now I get personal. What happened to your face?"

I took a deep breath. "If I tell you the truth, does a lecture go with it?"

Curt wouldn't commit himself. "What happened?" he insisted.

I wished the elevator would stop at another floor. But when I looked up at the indicator, there were no other lights showing. I had no choice. I told Curt in the dead tone of a Jack Webb, "I raped my ex-wife, and her boyfriend beat me up."

Curt said nothing. He was visibly shocked. "You have become a very sick man, Stephen," he finally decided.

"I know."

"Maybe you should take a vacation?"

"No. I need my work."

"Maybe *I* should take a vacation," Curt ventured.

I turned to Curt, noticing him really for the first time that day. "What's the matter?" I asked.

He sighed. "Karen and I have been picking at each other."

I could not imagine Curt and his wife Karen picking at each other. I thought that theirs was an ideal—if square—marriage. "Is it serious?" I asked.

"I don't think so." Curt pressed his nose down against his pursed lips. But then he seemed to reconsider. "I don't know, though. Karen may be a victim of too much exposure to a sick society."

The elevator stopped at our floor, but Curt seemed reluctant to leave our conversation just there. "Do you want to talk about it?" I asked, gently ushering him out the doors and down the corridor toward our office suite.

"I was brushing my teeth the other night, getting ready for bed," Curt began, "when I smelled something burning." He stopped and looked about furtively, his voice dropping to a whisper and his nostrils quivering as if the smell were still omnipresent. "I walked into the bedroom and there was Karen smoking . . ." he paused melodramatically, "pot."

I all but snickered. "That's not so bad."

"I will not have my wife," said Curt rhetorically, "smoking pot in my house."

I opened the door to our office suite, shaking my head. "I don't think you have a problem, Curt."

Curt's eyes flitted about the waiting room. "We'll talk about it later," he said in a low voice and fled into his office.

One of the women in the waiting room ran up to me tearfully. "I have to see you right away, Mr. Blume," she cried.

It was Mrs. Cramer. She seemed to have aged ten years since she had last walked out of my office announcing her reconciliation with her psychiatrist husband. "Mrs. Cramer," I held her hand and comforted her, "what seems to be the trouble?"

"My husband did it again," she wailed. "He ran off with another cockamamie stewardess."

"I'm sorry." I patted her hand. "Just let me make a few calls and I'll be right with you."

And so it was all dissolving right in front of me. I had the feeling that all the married couples in the United States needed two or three weeks in Venice to cool off. Certainly, if all the marriages that were in trouble faced up to the truth, the courts would not be able to handle the traffic.

Several weeks passed. My bruises healed, but my heart was broken. Arlene tried to help, but she couldn't. One Saturday morning she came over to my room. I was still in bed. "What do you want to do?" she announced briskly, sitting on the edge of the bed.

I had all the enthusiasm of a wet blanket. "I think I'll read, Arlene," I said.

"Do you want me to go?" she asked sullenly.

"No, you can stay." I turned the page of the Vonnegut paperback I was reading. "But I just want to read."

Arlene sat there restless. She didn't quite know what to do. She heaved a sigh of desperation. "What do you have to read?" she asked.

"I don't know." I pointed to the night table. "Did you read the new Updike?"

She shook her head and cringed. "Do you have any magazines?"

"Yeah. *Time. Esquire . . .*"

Arlene picked up a copy of *Esquire* and leafed through it quickly. "I don't want to read," she decided. "Maybe I'll go."

She stood up, waiting for me to stop her, but I didn't. What for? She leaned over and kissed me warmly, flashing her joggling tits before me. I felt warm and friendly toward her—but not sexy. I kissed her on the forehead.

This hurt Arlene. "Why don't you join a monastery?" she said bitterly.

"It's not out of the question," I agreed. Then I sat up and put my hands on her shoulders. "Arlene," I said, "go home. Find a good man."

"You really love her, don't you?"

"Yes."

"And you really feel sorry for yourself, don't you?"

"Yes."

Arlene stood up again and smoothed out her dress. "Goodbye, Blume," she said.

They always call me Blume when they get pissed off. I got up and took Arlene in my arms and hugged her. She hugged me back. And she was crying, the mascara running down her cheeks. "I didn't use you. We used each other," I said, tucking her under the chin. "And it was fun."

She sniffled, looked me in the eyes bravely, and turned around and walked out of my life.

And so I spent my days at the office divorcing people, and I spent my nights alone in bed reading books. I didn't see or hear from Nina or Elmo. I was a wren, a slug, a jellyfish. Then it turned around. As only life can turn it all around. I was getting ready to leave my office one night when my aged secretary, Louise, wheezed in. "Mr. Blume, there's a man to see you."

I checked my watch. It was after hours. "I'm sorry I can't see him, Louise," I said, "I'm going home."

"He says he's a friend of yours."

I wondered for a moment if it could be possible. "Does he have a beard?"

"Yes."

I went to the door and sneaked a peek, then opened it wide and called out, "Come in, my friend."

Elmo sidled in, looking around my office, absorbing the fact that there was a facet to my existence he had never known before.

Louise couldn't figure out what was happening. "See you in the morning, Louise," I said, to signal that she could go.

"Good night, Mr. Blume."

"Good night, Louise." She left my office, shutting the door behind her.

As always, I was genuinely glad to see Elmo. He jolted me pleasurably back into the concept of stationary time. Even the threads he wore were the same as the last time I had seen him—the same pants, the same red shirt, the same desert boots. "How's it going?" I asked.

"Nothin' to it," he shrugged.

164

I suddenly began to sing to the tune of that old Weavers record: "Good night, Louise . . .

Good night, Louise . . ."

and soon Elmo joined in with his twangy bass and we were singing together:

"Good night, Louise . . .

Louise, Louise . . .

Good night . . ."

"Hey," I broke off, "you want a drink?" And headed for the liquor cabinet behind my desk.

I expected to hear a yes or no. Instead I heard: "Your old lady is pregnant."

I stopped cold, frozen in my tracks.

"Just got the old rabbit test," Elmo continued.

I was in a state of shock. Mechanically I managed to open the cabinet, find two glasses on the tray, remove a bottle of Scotch, and pour two healthy shots. I took a quick slug of mine before turning around and asking hoarsely, "How can she be pregnant?"

Elmo shrugged. "Some guy knocked her up."

"But we could never have kids," I said disbelievingly.

"The lady," Elmo repeated, measuring out his words, "has got a baby cooking in the oven."

I handed him his drink. "How do you know it's my baby?"

Elmo laughed. "Only Catholics and rapists don't use birth control."

"Is she going to have the baby?"

Elmo held up his drink as if in silent toast. "She can't wait," he said, and drank to it.

I drank with him. But I was too excited, confused, overwhelmed, to find my bearings. And there was one important point I couldn't grasp yet at all. "Does Nina know you're here?"

"No," Elmo said. "But that's okay. I'll tell her."

My body was in a state of vibrant, tingling shock. "I'm shaking," I grinned sheepishly.

"I'm splitting," Elmo grinned back.

"Finish your drink," I said quickly.

"Splitting L.A.," Elmo explained, taking another sip.

"Why? What about Nina?"

"She knows," Elmo reassured me. "See, I don't work. You know that. And I don't see Nina and the baby living in my pickup truck."

"I'll support you," I promised generously. "It's my baby," I added proudly.

"I could handle that," said Elmo, "but I don't think Nina could."

I was curious. "Does she have a belly yet?"

Elmo nodded. "If you put your head down there and listen, you can just barely make something out."

I couldn't get over it. "It's a miracle," I said, still catching my breath. I picked up the Scotch bottle, freshened our drinks, and then all but collapsed on my office couch. "Wow!" I held the bottle in the air like a celebrant in a winning Super Bowl team's locker room.

Mike, the cleaning man, poked his head into my office doorway, pail, dustpan, and broom in hand. "Oh. Sorry, Mr. Blume. I thought you were gone," he said, beginning to retreat.

"That's okay, Mike," I waved him into the office, "you can do your work." Mike was staring at the bottle in my hand. "I'm going to be a father," I explained.

"That's wonderful," Mike congratulated me. "Wonderful." And he started emptying the ashtrays.

Elmo joined me on the couch so that he wouldn't be in Mike's way. "What's Nina going to do if you go?" I asked him. Then I proceeded to answer my own question with an entreaty. "You can't go, Elmo," I pleaded.

"It's time to split," Elmo insisted.

"But what's going to happen?"

We both picked up our legs so that Mike could sweep under them.

"I'm heading north to see what evil lurks in the heart of man," Elmo said, as if he were already no longer interested in Nina, me, or any of the problems relating to us. "You go see your old lady," he counseled.

"But she's your old lady, Elmo."

Elmo sighed. "I'm not sure where she's at . . ."

"Do you think," I asked hopefully, "she'd marry me again?"

I noticed Mike staring at me, his mouth open. It was too complicated to try to explain to him—or anyone else. Hell, I still didn't quite understand what was happening myself. Elmo hadn't answered my question, so I repeated it. "Just your opinion, Elmo, do you think there's a chance Nina might remarry me?"

"Stephen," Elmo rose, "I cannot speak for the lady." He held out his hand. "So long, friend."

I jumped to my feet. I held his hand and looked into sad, warm eyes. "Are you really going?"

"I'll drop you a postcard," he said in answer. And he gave me a bear hug. I was so moved I began to cry.

"Why are you going, the real reason, Elmo?"

"Time to split." He backed toward the door, his hand in the air.

"How will you live?"

"Nothin' to it."

He turned around and walked through the waiting room and out of our office suite. I heard the sound of his footsteps echoing along the marble floor all the way to the elevator.

I took a Kleenex from my top drawer and wiped my eyes with it. "That's some guy," I told Mike. "He's something else."

And I felt instantly bereft. As if I had lost my best friend.

That was the last time I saw Elmo. He dropped me a postcard about three months later. It had a photo of a gorilla on one side. All it said on the other side was:

"Nothin' to it."

I didn't know what to do. I was afraid to see Nina. Afraid to find out what she was going to do. But I was no longer depressed. And finally one sunny day I drove out to Venice, to the County Welfare Office where Nina worked. I parked on the lot, feeling a pang when I saw Nina's yellow VW. I hadn't seen it for months. And I went over and tapped it on the hood the way one pats a familiar horse.

I walked in through the front entrance, past the information desk and the general waiting area, down to the corridor where Nina's cubicle was. A Mexican woman was leaving

Nina's office in tears as I stuck my head in the doorway.

"What's up, Blume?" Nina said sharply. She was wearing a maternity outfit. But since she was sitting behind the desk I couldn't tell how pregnant she had become.

I looked after the Mexican woman. "I think I came on the wrong day," I said.

"We get that every day," Nina said very businesslike. And just as businesslike, she rose, revealing a bulging belly which she patted. "The baby is due October the nineteenth, and it's definitely yours, Blume," she said.

"I know," I grinned happily.

She sat down again behind her desk and picked up some forms and riffled through them. "So what do you want?" she asked.

"I want . . ." I began, "I want to know how you are."

"I feel good," she laid down the papers. "I wanted Elmo to leave. It wasn't going anywhere, and it was only going to get more complicated."

"I'd like to support the baby," I volunteered.

"If I need it, I'll take it." She mulled it over. "But that's tomorrow," she decided, deferring such a decision.

"Let me pay the doctor bills," I offered.

"I have coverage from the job."

"You seem very together about the baby."

"I am."

I couldn't help it. It eked out of me like air from a leaking balloon. I had manfully contained myself until then. "I love you," I said.

Nina picked up the papers on her desk. "See you, Blume," she said.

And I left. But I was feeling better. Nina even let me call her now and then. She was always very businesslike. But she did give progress reports. I started to drive to the house to see her several times, but I felt it would blow things. So I wrote her letters. Love letters. Or love prayers. Like:

Nina, of course I love you. Maybe I'm being romantic but I think the baby is telling us something. Let me see you. See if I've changed. Or if I haven't changed, maybe *we* have. Marry me. Let me marry you.

But I would get no answers. In our phone conversations

Nina would never even allude to my letters. But I began to get feelings, to sense vibes. And there came a night when Nina was six months pregnant that I risked everything—or the little that I had, which was everything to me.

I drove up the Canyon to the house. I pulled in, dimming my lights. And then I crept to the window, the window from which I first saw Nina and Elmo together, and then again like a Peeping Tom, I looked in the window.

Nina was in the living room, a fire blazing in the fireplace, curled up on the sofa, strumming her guitar. Only now it was a little awkward for her to hold the instrument. But still she seemed to be having a good time, to be contented, her belly swelling under the Ralph Abernathy poor people's loose-fitting overalls she was wearing. The tune she was strumming was:

"Sitting around doing nothing . . .
Sitting around going nowhere . . .
Sitting around with our family . . ."

I could hear it loud and clear. I was pleased with how much her guitar-playing had improved.

Suddenly, she stopped and grimaced pleasurably. And then she patted her swollen belly beneath the guitar. "If you're a boy, kid," I heard her say, "you'd better learn to respect women. And if you're a girl, kid, I'm going to teach you to respect yourself."

She put her guitar back into position and began to play "Sitting around doing nothing" again. And, this time, unconsciously I quietly hummed along outside the window. Or was it unconscious? All I can recall is yearning to be a part of the serenity within. My Nina. Elmo's music. Our baby.

I did not realize that I had given myself away until I saw Nina coming to the window. I ducked down and began to creep away. But too late. The window opened and Nina, recognizing me even from the overhead side rear, called out, "Blume?"

"Yes." I got up, dusting myself off.

"What do you want?"

"I wanted to see how the baby was coming along."

"I don't believe you."

"I wanted to see you."

"Why didn't you say so?"

"I'm not too confident around you any more."

Nina laughed and closed the window. She opened the door and came into the garden. "I won't call the police," she said, approaching me. "I want to talk to you, anyway."

I was immediately suspicious. "Are you high?"

"No. I was thinking about your offer. The money?"

"Good," I said. And I meant it. I wanted desperately to contribute to the welfare of the baby in any possible way.

"I haven't decided yet," she cautioned me. "But I may take you up on it. I want to spend a lot of time with the baby."

"Sure."

"Also, I think you have a right to be in on the kid's name."

I was pleased. I had never allowed myself to even consider that possibility.

"I like Molly for a girl," Nina continued, "and Chester for a boy."

"Chester?" I crinkled up my nose.

"After Elmo's uncle."

"I like Molly," I said, "but I don't like Chester."

Nina smiled. "Would you rather go for Elmo?"

I smiled back. "It wouldn't bother me."

"I really like Chester."

"What about Chet?" I bargained.

"I don't like it," Nina shook her head.

"Let me think about Chester."

"Okay," Nina said. "You better go."

I followed her to the door. In ill-fitting overalls with a bulging belly she was the most beautiful woman I had ever seen. "You're remarkable," I said.

"No, I'm not."

"Where are we?" I asked.

"Nowhere."

"Not even in limbo?"

"We're where we are. Good night, Blume."

"Good night."

She closed the door and I walked back to my car, surprised that my shirt was wet, realizing that it had begun to rain gently while I was in the garden talking to Nina. I looked up to the sky, the rain hitting my eyes, and prayed that Nina didn't catch cold.

I didn't see Nina again for a month. I called her once, though, to say Chester as a name was fine with me. Perfectly fine. Otherwise, I was just waiting for something to happen. I didn't know exactly what it was until one hot summer afternoon Louise knocked on my door and announced, "Mr. Blume, your wife is here to see you."

I was taken aback. "My wife?"

"Yes," Louise said nervously.

"Is that what she said? Wife?"

"No. No. She just said, tell Mr. Blume that Nina Blume wants to see him."

"Send her in," I said. And explained to Louise. "She's my ex-wife."

"I see," said Louise. But she was still nervous.

I was surprised at what walked in through the door. I never could imagine Nina that fat. She seemed ready to give birth to the baby immediately.

"You're almost there," I said.

"I'm going to quit the job," Nina said, as she sat down on the couch. "At least, temporarily."

"Right." I sat down beside her.

"And I may take you up on the money thing."

"It's yours."

"No strings?"

"No strings."

"You write a lot of letters."

"I'm in love."

"I'm beginning to believe you," she said quietly. "I still think about you."

I didn't want to spoil anything. I didn't say anything.

"You can talk, Blume," Nina smiled.

"What should we do?" I asked.

"I don't want you to write any more letters. I get the message. I want time to think. I don't want to feel any pressure."

"No more letters," I promised.

"But it's got to be your decision, too."

"My decision was made a long time ago."

"Not that," Nina shook her head. "If we get together again—and I said *if*—it's got to be equal. No games."

"No more letters," I repeated. "No more games," I added. "Just tell me what I should do."

Nina held up her hand. "Wait," she said. "Just wait. Let me think. Let me work it out. I'm beginning to want to see you again. I don't know why. I'm not sure why. But that's how it is. Maybe we shouldn't have ended it the way we did. *I* did. I don't know. But I still think about you. Sometimes I don't want to. But I do. Elmo knew about it." She smiled. "He said you were part of my memory bank."

"Elmo," I said, "is part of my memory bank."

"Yes," Nina nodded. And we both bowed our heads as if in instant tribute. Nina looked up first. "Why don't you go to Venice?"

"Myself?"

"Or anywhere," Nina rushed on. "It's just that I know you like Venice. But give me a few weeks to think."

"I want to be here when the baby is born."

"You will," she assured me. "I want just a few weeks without you in the same place. So I can feel free. Really free."

I went to my desk and pressed the intercom. "Louise," I said into it, "order me a round-trip flight for Venice. Venice, Italy. For tomorrow, if you can get it."

Nina stood up and came to my desk. "We'll talk in a few weeks. Have a nice time, Blume."

I reached out and touched her belly. "Okay, Blume," I said.

And that was the last I saw of her. I came to Venice. I've been here three weeks. No letters. No games. A lot of sight-seeing. Guidecca Island. The Ducal Palace. The Basilica. Campanile Tower. A lot of time to think. A lot of time to write. A lot of time to watch pigeons. A lot of time to drink espresso. A lot of time to figure out the linguistic quirks of waiters.

Mostly, though, as I say, sitting around the old café. Sit-

172

ting around the Piazza San Marco. Sitting around drinking espresso. Writing on these notebook pages.

They have put up a bandstand again in the Piazza today. They're having a concert, which will begin any minute now. The orchestra is in position. The conductor is on the podium. He's stretched his arms, he's given the beat, and the orchestra has begun to play the overture from *Tristan und Isolde*.

I want to listen.

So I'll close this notebook now. Tomorrow I go home, anyway. I am not certain of anything. I think there is a chance for Nina and me. There has to be. But then again, I don't know . . .

Postscript

As the music swelled, I looked out toward the Arcades in the corner of the Piazza. And I saw a vision: a woman approaching who looked like Nina. Was it a dream, or was it a reality? I couldn't tell. I had to find out. I got up and started running toward that figure. And soon I could see the figure was scanning the Piazza looking for me. It was Nina. I ran like I've never run before. I leaped like a gazelle in the *Song of Songs*, I pranced like a reindeer in a Christmas Special, I streaked like a Harold Lloyd in a silent comedy. I reached Nina like a Maury Wills flying into third standing up.

"Hi Blume," Nina smiled.

"Hi Blume," I smiled back. And took her in my arms and held her sweet eight-month pregnant baby-filled body. Then I patted her belly. "Let's get married."

"No."

"But that'll make the kid a bastard."

Nina shook her head. "There's no such thing."

We sat down at my table, and my usual pencil-line-mustached waiter came over. At the sight of Nina he was all smiles. As if he had spent three weeks worrying about me.

"It is nice to see your wife with you, *signore*," he said in perfect English.

"She's not my wife."

This confused him. *"Scusi?"*

"She is the mother of my child."

For the first time he really lost his cool. *"Bene, bene, signore,"* he stuttered.

I was delighted. I turned to Nina. "What'll you have?"

There was a strange look on her face. One I had never seen before. "What?" she asked.

"What do you want to drink?" I repeated. Then I read the look instinctively. "What's the matter?"

"The baby," Nina said. She was holding her belly, breathing deeply, but smiling.

I was frantic. The orchestra was reaching a climax, Wagner at his most sublime. And that didn't help any, either.

I shouted to the waiter, "Where's the hospital? *Ospedale?"*

"Scusi, signore?"

I stood up and shook the son-of-a-bitch. *"You understand English. My wife is having a baby!"*

"Ah," he nodded, "the baby . . ."

"I'm not your wife," Nina corrected me, despite her pain.

The waiter pointed off in the direction of the Ducal Palace, shouting the necessary instructions after me. For we had already begun to walk there, my arm tenderly around Nina, while the music soared to its finale.

Molly is seven months old now. She is a happy little bastard. Nina and I are happy, too. She is going back to work soon, she says. And I don't take anyone or anything for granted any more. I am still divorcing people. But something is different for us.

We're in love. It's a miracle. Love is a miracle.

Yes.